THE DRIVER'S SEAT

Muriel Spark

A NEW DIRECTIONS BOOK

Published by arrangement with Dame Muriel Spark and her agent Georges Borchardt, Inc., New York.

Manufactured in the United States of America
First published as a New Directions Bibelot in 1994. Republished as New Directions Paperbook 1284 in 2014 (ISBN 978-0-8112-2301-0)
Design by Erik Rieselbach

Library of Congress Cataloging-in-Publication Data
The driver's seat / Muriel Spark
p. cm.
ISBN 978-0-8112-1271-7
1. Women—Travel—Italy—Fiction 2. Murder—Italy—Fiction.
I. Title
PR6037. P29D7   1994
823'.914—dc20   93-50803

10 9 8 7 6 5 4 3

New Directions books are published for James Laughlin
by New Directions Publishing Corporation
80 Eighth Avenue, New York 10011

Chapter One

A ND THE MATERIAL doesn't stain,' the salesgirl says. 'Doesn't stain?'

'It's the new fabric,' the salesgirl says. 'Specially treated. Won't mark. If you spill like a bit of ice-cream or a drop of coffee, like, down the front of this dress it won't hold the stain.'

The customer, a young woman, is suddenly tearing at the fastener at the neck, pulling at the zip of the dress. She is saying, 'Get this thing off me. Off me, at once.'

The salesgirl shouts at the customer who, up to now, has been delighted with the bright coloured dress. It is patterned with green and purple squares on a white background, with blue spots within the green squares, cyclamen spots within the purple. This dress has not been a successful line; other dresses in the new stainless fabric have sold, but this, of which three others, identical but for sizes, hang in the back storeroom awaiting the drastic reductions of next week's sale, has been too vivid for most customers' taste. But the customer who now steps speedily out of it, throwing it on the floor with the utmost irritation, had almost smiled with satisfaction when she had tried it on. She had said, 'That's my dress.' The salesgirl had said it needed taking up at the hem. 'All right,' the customer had said, 'but I need it for tomorrow.' 'We can't do it before Friday, I'm sorry,' the salesgirl had said. 'Oh, I'll do it myself, then,' the customer had said, and turned round to admire it sideways in the long mirror. 'It's a good fit. Lovely colours,' she said.

'And it doesn't stain,' the salesgirl had said, with her eye wandering to another unstainable and equally unsaleable summer dress which evidently she hoped, now, to offer the satisfied customer.

'Doesn't stain?'

The customer has flung the dress aside.

The salesgirl shouts, as if to assist her explanation. 'Specially treated fabric ... If you spill like a drop of sherry you just wipe it off. Look, Miss, you're tearing the neck.'

'Do you think I spill things on my clothes?' the customer shrieks. 'Do I look, as if I don't eat properly?'

'Miss, I only remarked on the fabric, that when you tell me you're going abroad for your vacation, there is always the marks that you pick up on your journey. Don't treat our clothes like that if you please. Miss, I only said stain-resisting and then you carry on, after you liked it.'

'Who asked you for a stain-resisting dress?' the customer shouts, getting quickly, with absolute purpose, into her own blouse and skirt.

'You liked the colours, didn't you?' shouts the girl. 'What difference does it make, so it resists stains, if you liked the fabric before you knew?'

The customer picks up her bag and goes to the door almost at a run, while two other salesgirls and two other customers gasp and gape. At the door she turns to look back and says, with a look of satisfaction at her own dominance over the situation with an undoubtable excuse, 'I won't be insulted!'

She walks along the broad street, scanning the windows for the dress she needs, the necessary dress. Her lips are slightly parted; she, whose lips are usually pressed together with the daily disapprovals of the accountants' office where she has worked continually, except for the months of illness, since she was eighteen, that is to say, for sixteen years and some months. Her lips, when she does not speak or eat, are normally pressed together like the ruled line of a balance sheet, marked straight with her old-fashioned lipstick, a final and a judging mouth, a precision instrument, a detail-warden of a mouth; she has five girls under her and two men. Over her are two women and five men. Her immediate superior had given her the afternoon off, in kindness, Friday afternoon. 'You've got your packing to do, Lise. Go home, pack and rest.' She had resisted. 'I don't need a rest. I've got all this work to finish. Look—all this.' The superior, a fat small man, looked at her with frightened eyeglasses. Lise smiled and bent her head over her desk. 'It can wait till you get back,' said the man, and when she looked up at him he showed courage and defiance in his rimless spectacles. Then she had begun to laugh hysterically. She finished laughing and started crying all in a flood, while a flurry at the other desks, the jerky backward movements of her little fat superior, conveyed to her that she had done again what she had not done for five years. As she ran to the lavatory she shouted to the whole office who somehow or other were trying to follow or help her. 'Leave me alone! It doesn't matter. What does it matter?' Half an hour later they said, 'You need a good holiday, Lise. You need your vacation.' 'I'm going to have it,' she said, 'I'm going to have the time of my life,' and she had looked at the two men and five girls under her, and at her quivering superior, one by one, with her lips straight as a line which could cancel them all out completely.

Now, as she walks along the street after leaving the shop, her lips are slightly parted as if to receive a secret flavour. In fact her nostrils and eyes are a fragment more open than usual, imperceptibly but thoroughly they accompany her parted lips in one mission, the sensing of the dress that she must get.

She swerves in her course at the door of a department store and enters. Resort Department: she has seen the dress. A lemon-yellow top with a skirt patterned in bright V's of orange, mauve and blue. 'Is it made of that stain-resisting material?' she asks when she has put it on and is looking at herself in the mirror. 'Stain-resisting? I don't know. Madam. It's a washable cotton, but if I were you I'd have it dry-cleaned. It might shrink.' Lise laughs, and the girl says, 'I'm afraid we haven't anything really stain-resisting. I've never heard of anything like that.' Lise makes her mouth into a straight line. Then she says, 'I'll have it.' Meanwhile she is pulling off a hanger a summer coat with narrow stripes, red and white, with a white collar; very quickly she tries it on over the new dress. 'Of course, the two don't go well together,' says the salesgirl. 'You'd have to see them on separate.'

Lise does not appear to listen. She studies herself. This way and that, in the mirror of the fitting room. She lets the coat hang open over the dress. Her lips part, and her eyes narrow; she breathes for a moment as in a trance.

The salesgirl says, 'You can't really see the coat at its best, Madam, over that frock.'

Lise appears suddenly to hear her, opening her eyes and closing her lips. The girl is saying, 'You won't be able to wear them together, but it's a lovely coat, over a plain dress, white or navy, or for the evenings ...'

'They go very well together,' Lise says, and taking off the coat she hands it carefully to the girl. 'I'll have it; also, the dress. I can take up the hem myself.' She reaches for her blouse and skirt and says to the girl, 'Those colours of the dress and the coat are absolutely right for me. Very natural colours.'

The girl, placating, says, 'Oh, it's how you feel in things yourself, Madam, isn't it? It's you's got to wear them.' Lise buttons her blouse disapprovingly. She follows the girl to the shop-floor, pays the bill, waits for the change and, when the girl hands her first the change then the large bag of heavy paper containing her new purchases, she opens the top of the bag enough to enable her to peep inside, to put in her hand and tear a corner of the tissue paper which enfolds each garment. She is obviously making sure she is being handed the right garments. The girl is about to speak, probably to say, 'Everything all right?' or 'Thank you. Madam, goodbye,' or even, 'Don't worry; everything's there all right.' But Lise speaks first; she says, 'The colours go together perfectly. People here in the North are ignorant of colours. Conservative; old-fashioned. If only you knew! These colours are a natural blend for me. Absolutely natural.' She does not wait for a reply; she does not turn towards the lift, she turns, instead, towards the down escalator, purposefully making her way through a short lane of dresses that hang in their stands.

She stops abruptly at the top of the escalator and looks back, then smiles as if she sees and hears what she had expected. The salesgirl, thinking her customer is already on the escalator out of sight, out of hearing, has turned to another black-frocked salesgirl. 'All those colours together!' she is saying. 'Those incredible colours! She said they were perfectly natural. Natural! Here in the North, she said ...' Her voice stops as she sees that Lise is looking and hearing. The girl affects to be fumbling with a dress on the rack and to be saying something else without changing her expression too noticeably. Lise laughs aloud and descends the escalator.

'Well, enjoy yourself Lise,' says the voice on the telephone. 'Send me a card.'

'Oh, of course,' Lise says, and when she has hung up she laughs heartily. She does not stop. She goes to the wash-basin and fills a glass of water, which she drinks, gurgling, then another, and still nearly choking she drinks another. She has stopped laughing, and now breathing heavily says to the mute telephone, 'Of course. Oh, of course.' Still heaving with exhaustion she pulls out the hard wall-seat which adapts to a bed and takes off her shoes, placing them beside the bed. She puts the large carrier-bag containing her new coat and dress in a cupboard beside her suitcase which is already packed. She places her hand-bag on the lamp-shelf beside the bed and lies down.

Her face is solemn as she lies, at first staring at the brown pinewood door as if to see beyond it. Presently her breathing becomes normal. The room is meticulously neat. It is a one-room flat in an apartment house. Since it was put up the designer has won prizes for his interiors, he has become known throughout the country and far beyond and is now no longer to be obtained by landlords of moderate price. The lines of the room are pure; space is used as a pattern in itself, circumscribed by the dexterous pinewood outlines that ensued from the designer's ingenuity and austere taste when he was young, unknown, studious and strict-principled. The company that owns the apartment house knows the worth of these pinewood interiors. Pinewood alone is now nearly as scarce as the architect himself, but the law, so far, prevents them from raising the rents very much. The tenants have long leases. Lise moved in when the house was new, ten years ago. She has added very little to the room; very little is needed, for the furniture is all fixed, adaptable to various uses, and stackable. Stacked into a panel are six folding chairs, should the tenant decide to entertain six for dinner. The writing desk extends to a dining table, and when the desk is not in use it, too, disappears into the pinewood wall, its bracket-lamp hingeing outward and upward to form a wall-lamp. The bed is by day a narrow seat with overhanging bookcases; by night it swivels out to accommodate the sleeper. Lise has put down a patterned rug from Greece. She has fitted a hopsack covering on the seat of the divan. Unlike the other tenants she has not put unnecessary curtains in the window; her flat is not closely overlooked and in summer she keeps the Venetian blinds down over the windows and slightly opened to let in the light. A small pantry-kitchen adjoins this room. Here, too, everything is contrived to fold away into the dignity of unvarnished pinewood. And in the bathroom as well, nothing need be seen, nothing need be left lying about. The bed-supports, the door, the window frame, the hanging cupboard, the storage space, the shelves, the desk that extends, the tables that stack—they are made of such pine-wood as one may never see again in a modest bachelor apartment. Lise keeps her flat as clean-lined and clear to return to after her work as if it were uninhabited. The swaying tall pines among the litter of cones on the forest floor have been subdued into silence and into obedient bulks.

Lise breathes as if sleeping, deeply tired, but her eye-slits open from time to time. Her hand moves to her brown leather bag on the lamp-shelf and she raises herself, pulling the bag towards her. She leans on one elbow and empties the contents on the bed. She lifts them one by one, checking carefully, and puts them back; there is a folded envelope from the travel agency containing her air ticket, a powder compact, a lipstick, a comb. There is a bunch of keys. She smiles at them and her lips are parted. There are six keys on the steel ring, two Yale door-keys, a key that might belong to a functional cupboard or drawer, a small silver-metal key of the type commonly belonging to zip-fastened luggage, and two tarnished car-keys. Lise takes the car-keys off the ring and lays them aside; the rest go back in her bag. Her passport, in its transparent plastic envelope, goes back in her bag. With straightened lips she prepares for her departure the next day. She unpacks the new coat and dress and hangs them on hangers.

Next morning she puts them on. When she is ready to leave she dials a number on the telephone and looks at herself in the mirror which has not yet been concealed behind the pinewood panels which close upon it. The voice answers and Lise touches her pale brown hair as she speaks. 'Margot, I'm just off now,' Lise says. 'I'll put your car-keys in an envelope and I'll leave them downstairs with the door-keeper. All right?'

The voice says, 'Thanks. Have a good holiday. Have a good time. Send me a card.'

'Yes, of course, Margot.'

'Of course,' Lise says when she has replaced the receiver. She takes an envelope from a drawer, writes a name on it, puts the two car-keys in it and seals the envelope. Then she telephones for a taxi, lifts her suitcase out to the landing, fetches her hand-bag and the envelope, and leaves the flat.

When she reaches the street floor, she stops at the windows of the porter's wood-lined cabin. Lise rings the bell and waits. No one appears, but the taxi has pulled up outside. Lise shouts to the driver, 'I'm just coming!' and indicates her suitcase which the taxi-driver fetches. While he is stacking it in the front of the cab a woman with a brown overall comes up behind Lise. 'You want me, Miss?'

Lise turns quickly to face the woman. She has the envelope in her hand and is about to speak when the woman says, 'Well, well, my goodness, what colours!' She is looking at Lise's red and white striped coat, unbuttoned, and the vivid dress beneath, the purple, orange and blue V-patterns of the skirt and the yellow top. The woman laughs hugely as one who has nothing to gain by suppressing her amusement, she laughs and opens the pinewood door into the porter's office; there she slides open the window panel and laughs aloud in Lise's face. She says, 'Are you going to join a circus?' Then again she throws back her head, looking down through half-closed lids at Lise's clothes, and gives out the high, hacking cough-like ancestral laughter of the streets, holding her breasts in her hands to spare them the shake-up. Lise says, with quiet dignity, 'You are insolent.' But the woman laughs again, now no longer spontaneously but with spiteful and deliberate noise, forcing the evident point that Lise habitually is mean with her tips, or perhaps never tips the porter at all.

Lise walks quietly out to the cab, still holding in her hand the envelope which contains the car-keys. She looks at this envelope as she goes, but whether she has failed to leave it at the door-keeper's desk by intention, or whether through the distraction of the woman's laughter, one could not tell from her serene face with lips slightly parted. The woman comes to the street door emitting noise like a brown container of laughing-gas until the taxi is out of her scope.

Chapter Two

LISE IS THIN. Her height is about five-foot-six. Her hair is pale brown, probably tinted, a very light streaked lock sweeping from the middle of her hair-line to the top of her crown; her hair is cut short at the sides and back, and is styled high. She might be as young as twenty-nine or as old as thirty-six, but hardly younger, hardly older. She has arrived at the airport; she has paid the taxi-driver quickly and with an expression of abstract eagerness to be somewhere else. Likewise, with the porter, while he takes her bag and follows her to the desk to have it weighed-in. She seems not to see him.

There are two people in front of her. Lise's eyes are widely spaced, blue-grey and dull. Her lips are a straight line. She is neither good-looking nor bad-looking. Her nose is short and wider than it will look in the likeness constructed partly by the method of identikit, partly by actual photography, soon to be published in the newspapers of four languages.

Lise looks at the two people in front of her, first a woman and then a man, swaying to one side and the other as she does so, either to discern in the half-faces visible to her someone she might possibly know, or else to relieve, by these movements and looks, some impatience she might feel.

When it comes to her turn she heaves her luggage on to the scale and pushes her ticket to the clerk as quickly as possible. While he examines it she turns to look at a couple who are now waiting behind her. She glances at both faces, then looks back to the clerk, regardless of their returning her stares and their unanimous perception of her bright-coloured clothes.

'Any hand-luggage?' says the clerk, peering over the top of the counter.

Lise simpers, placing the tips of her upper teeth over her lower lip, and draws in a little breath.

'Any hand-luggage?' The busy young official looks at her as much as to say, 'What's the matter with *you*?' And Lise answers in a voice different from the voice in which she yesterday spoke to the shop assistant when buying her lurid outfit, and has used on the telephone, and in which early this morning she spoke to the woman at the porter's desk; she now speaks in a little-girl tone which presumably is taken by those within hearing to be her normal voice even if a nasty one. Lise says, 'I only have my hand-bag with me. I believe in travelling light because I travel a lot and I know how terrible it is for one's neighbours on the plane when you have great huge pieces of hand-luggage taking up everybody's foot-room.'

The clerk, all in one gesture, heaves a sigh, purses his lips, closes his eyes, places his chin in his hands and his elbow on the desk. Lise turns round to address the couple behind her. She says, 'When you travel as much as I do you have to travel light, and I tell you, I nearly didn't bring any luggage at all, because you can get everything you want at the other end, so the only reason I brought that suitcase there is that the customs get suspicious if you come in and out without luggage. They think you're smuggling dope and diamonds under your blouse, so I packed the usual things for a holiday, but it was all quite unnecessary, as you get to understand when you've travelled about as you might say with experience in four languages over the years, and you know what you're doing—'

'Look, Miss,' the clerk says, pulling himself straight and stamping her ticket, 'you're holding up the people behind you. We're busy.'

Lise turns away from the bewildered-looking couple to face the clerk as he pushes her ticket and boarding card towards her. 'Boarding card,' says the clerk. 'Your flight will be called in twenty-five minutes' time. Next please.'

Lise grabs the papers and moves away as if thinking only of the next formality of travel. She puts the ticket in her bag, takes out her passport, slips the boarding card inside it, and makes straight towards the passport boxes. And it is almost as if, satisfied that she has successfully registered the fact of her presence at the airport among the July thousands there, she has fulfilled a small item of a greater purpose. She goes to the emigration official and joins the queue and submits her passport. And now, having received her passport back in her hand, she is pushing through the gate into the departure lounge. She walks to the far end, then turns and walks back. She is neither good-looking nor bad-looking. Her lips are slightly parted. She stops to look at the departures chart, then walks on. The people around her are mostly too occupied with their purchases and their flight-numbers to notice her, but some of those who sit beside their hand-luggage and children on the leather seats waiting for their flights to be called look at her as she walks past, noting without comment the lurid colours of her coat, red and white stripes, hanging loose over her dress, yellow-topped, with its skirt of orange, purple and blue. They look, as she passes, as they look also at those girls whose skirts are specially short, or those men whose tight-fitting shirts are patterned with flowers or are transparent. Lise is conspicuous among them only in the particular mixture of her colours, contrasting with the fact that her hem-line has been for some years an old-fashioned length, reaching just below her knees, as do the mild dresses of many other, but dingy, women travellers who teem in the departure lounge. Lise puts her passport into her hand-bag, and holds her boarding card.

She stops at the bookstall, looks at her watch and starts looking at the paperback stands. A white-haired, tall woman who has been looking through the hardback books piled up on a table, turns from them and, pointing to the paperbacks, says to Lise in English, 'Is there anything there predominantly pink or green or beige?'

'Excuse me?' says Lise politely, in a foreignly accented English, 'what is that you're looking for?'

'Oh,' the woman says, 'I thought you were American.'

'No, but I can speak four languages enough to make myself understood.'

'I'm from Johannesburg,' says the woman, 'and I have this house in Jo'burg and another at Sea Point on the Cape. Then my son, he's a lawyer, he has a flat in Jo'burg. In all our places we have spare bedrooms, that makes two green, two pink, three beige, and I'm trying to pick up books to match. I don't see any with just those pastel tints.'

'You want English books,' Lise says. 'I think you find English books on the front of the shop over there.'

'Well, I looked there and I don't find my shades. Aren't these English books here?'

Lise says 'No. In any case they're all very bright-coloured.' She smiles then, and with her lips apart starts to look swiftly through the paperbacks. She picks out one with bright green lettering on a white background with the author's name printed to look like blue lightning streaks. In the middle of the cover are depicted a brown boy and girl wearing only garlands of sunflowers. Lise pays for it, while the white-haired woman says, 'Those colours are too bright for me. I don't see anything.'

Lise is holding the book up against her coat, giggling merrily, and looking up to the woman as if to see if her purchase is admired.

'You going on holiday?' the woman says.

'Yes. My first after three years.'

'You travel much?'

'No. There is so little money. But I'm going to the South now. I went before, three years ago.'

'Well, I hope you have a good time. A very good time. You look very gay.'

The woman has large breasts, she is clothed in a pink summer coat and dress. She smiles and is amiable in this transient intimacy with Lise, and not even sensing in the least that very soon, after a day and a half of hesitancy, and after a long midnight call to her son, the lawyer in Johannesburg, who advises her against the action, she nevertheless will come forward and repeat all she remembers and all she does not remember, and all the details she imagines to be true and those that are true, in her conversation with Lise when she sees in the papers that the police are trying to trace who Lise is, and whom, if anyone, she met on her trip and what she had said. 'Very gay,' says this woman to Lise, indulgently, smiling all over Lise's vivid clothes.

'I look for a gay time,' Lise is saying.

'You got a young man?'

'Yes, I have my boy-friend!'

'He's not with you, then?'

'No. I'm going to find him. He's waiting for me. Maybe I should get him a gift at the duty-free shop.'

They are walking towards the departures chart. 'I'm going to Stockholm. I have three-quarters of an hour wait,' says the woman.

Lise looks at the chart as the amplified voice of the announcer hacks its way through the general din. Lise says, 'That's my flight. Boarding at Gate 14.' She moves off, her eyes in the distance as if the woman from Johannesburg had never been there. On her way to Gate 14 Lise stops to glance at a gift-stall. She looks at the dolls in folk-costume and at the corkscrews. Then she lifts up a paper-knife shaped like a scimitar, of brass-coloured metal with inset coloured stones. She removes it from its curved sheath and tests the blade and the point with deep interest. 'How much?' she asks the assistant who is at that moment serving someone else. The girl says impatiently aside to Lise, 'The price is on the ticket.'

'Too much. I can get it cheaper at the other end,' Lise says, putting it down.

'They're all fixed prices at the duty-free,' the girl calls after Lise as she walks away towards Gate 14.

A small crowd has gathered waiting for embarkation. More and more people straggle or palpitate, according to temperament, towards the group. Lise surveys her fellow-passengers, one by one, very carefully but not in a manner to provoke their attention. She moves and mingles as if with dreamy feet and legs, but quite plainly, from her eyes, her mind is not dreamy as she absorbs each face, each dress, each suit of clothes, all blouses, blue-jeans, each piece of hand-luggage, each voice which will accompany her on the flight now boarding at Gate 14.

Chapter Three

SHE WILL BE FOUND tomorrow morning dead from mul-tiple stab-wounds, her wrists bound with a silk scarf and her ankles bound with a man's necktie, in the grounds of an empty villa, in a park of the foreign city to which she is trav-elling on the flight now boarding at Gate 14.

Crossing the tarmac to the plane Lise follows, with her quite long stride, closely on the heels of the fellow-passenger whom she appears finally to have chosen to adhere to. This is a rosy-faced, sturdy young man of about thirty; he is dressed in a dark business suit and carries a black brief-case. She follows him purposefully, careful to block the path of any other trav-eller whose aimless hurry might intervene between Lise and this man. Meanwhile, closely behind Lise, almost at her side, walks a man who in turn seems anxious to be close to her. He tries unsuccessfully to catch her attention. He is bespectacled, half-smiling, young, dark, long-nosed and stooping. He wears a check shirt and beige corduroy trousers. A camera is slung over his shoulders and a coat over his arm.

Up the steps they go, the pink and shiny business man, Lise at his heels, and at hers the hungrier-looking man. Up the steps and into the plane. The air-hostess says good morning at the door while a steward farther up the aisle of the econ-omy class blocks the progress of the staggering file and helps a young woman with two young children to bundle their coats up on the rack. The way is clear at last. Lise's business man finds a seat next to the right-hand window in a three-seat row. Lise takes the middle seat next to him, on his left, while the lean hawk swiftly throws his coat and places his camera up on the rack and sits down next to Lise in the end seat.

Lise begins to fumble for her seat-belt. First she reaches down the right-hand side of her seat which adjoins that of the dark-suited man. At the same time she takes the left-hand section. But the right-hand buckle she gets hold of is that of her neighbour. It does not fit in the left-hand buckle as she tries to make it do. The dark-suited neighbour, fumbling also for his seat-belt, frowns as he seems to realize that she has the wrong part, and makes an unintelligible sound. Lise says, 'I think I've got yours.'

He fishes up the buckle that properly belongs to Lise's seat-belt. She says, 'Oh yes. I'm so sorry.' She giggles and he formally smiles and brings his smile to an end, now fastening his seat-belt intently and then looking out of the window at the wing of the plane, silvery with its rectangular patches.

Lise's left-hand neighbour smiles. The loudspeaker tells the passengers to fasten their seat-belts and refrain from smoking. Her admirer's brown eyes are warm, his smile, as wide as his forehead, seems to take up most of his lean face. Lise says, audibly above the other voices on the plane, 'You look like Red Riding-Hood's grandmother. Do you want to eat me up?'

The engines rev up. Her ardent neighbour's widened lips give out deep, satisfied laughter, while he slaps her knee in applause. Suddenly her other neighbour looks at Lise in alarm. He stares, as if recognizing her, with his brief-case on his lap, and his hand in the position of pulling out a batch of papers. Something about Lise, about her exchange with the man on her left, has caused a kind of paralysis in his act of fetching out some papers from his brief-case. He opens his mouth, gasping and startled, staring at her as if she is someone he has known and forgotten and now sees again. She smiles at him; it is a smile of relief and delight. His hand moves again, hurriedly putting back the papers that he had half-drawn out of his brief-case. He trembles as he unfastens his seat-belt and makes as if to leave his seat, grabbing his brief-case.

On the evening of the following day he will tell the police, quite truthfully, 'The first time I saw her was at the airport. Then on the plane. She sat beside me.'

'You never saw her before at any time? You didn't know her?'

'No, never.'

'What was your conversation on the plane?'

'Nothing. I moved my seat. I was afraid.'

'Afraid?'

'Yes, frightened. I moved to another seat, away from her.'

'What frightened you?'

'I don't know.'

'Why did you move your seat at that time?'

'I don't know. I must have sensed something.'

'What did she say to you?'

'Nothing much. She got her seat-belt mixed with mine. Then she was carrying on a bit with the man at the end seat.'

Now, as the plane taxis along the runway, he gets up. Lise and the man in the aisle seat look up at him, taken by surprise at the abruptness of his movements. Their seat-belts fasten them to their seats and they are unable immediately to make way for him, as he indicates that he wants to pass. Lise looks, for an instant, slightly senile, as if she felt, in addition to bewilderment, a sense of defeat or physical incapacity. She might be about to cry or protest against a pitiless frustration of her will. But an air-hostess, seeing the standing man, has left her post by the exit-door and briskly comes up the aisle to their seat. She says. 'The aircraft is taking off. Will you kindly remain seated and fasten your seat-belt?'

The man says, in a foreign accent, 'Excuse me, please. I wish to change.' He starts to squeeze past Lise and her companion.

The air-hostess, evidently thinking that the man has an urgent need to go to the lavatory, asks the two if they would mind getting up to let him pass and return to their seats as quickly as possible. They unfasten their belts, stand aside in the aisle, and he hurries up the plane with the air-hostess leading the way. But he does not get as far as the toilet cubicles. He stops at an empty middle seat upon which the people on either side, a white-haired fat man and a young girl, have dumped hand-luggage and magazines. He pushes himself past the woman who is seated on the outside seat and asks her to remove the luggage. He himself lifts it, shakily, his solid strength all gone. The air-hostess turns to remonstrate, but the two people have obediently made the seat vacant for him. He sits, fastens his seat-belt, ignoring the air-hostess, her reproving, questioning protests, and heaves a deep breath as if he had escaped from death by a small margin.

Lise and her companion have watched the performance. Lise smiles bitterly.

The dark man by her side says, 'What's wrong with him?'

'He didn't like us,' Lise says.

'What did we do to him?'

'Nothing. Nothing at all. He must be crazy. He must be nutty.'

The plane now comes to its brief halt before revving up for the take-off run. The engines roar and the plane is off, is rising and away. Lise says to her neighbour, 'I wonder who he is?'

'Some kind of a nut,' says the man. 'But it's all the better for us, we can get acquainted.' His stringy hand takes hers; he holds it tightly. 'I'm Bill,' he says. 'What's your name?'

'Lise.' She lets him grip her hand as if she hardly knows that he is holding it. She stretches her neck to see above the heads of the people in front, and says, 'He's sitting there reading the paper as if nothing had happened.'

The stewardess is handing out copies of newspapers. A steward who has followed her up the aisle stops at the seat where the dark-suited man has settled and is now tranquilly scanning the front page of his newspaper. The steward inquires if he is all right now, sir?

The man looks up with an embarrassed smile and shyly apologizes.

'Yes, fine. I'm sorry ...'

'Was there anything the matter, sir?'

'No, really. Please. I'm fine here, thanks. Sorry ... it was nothing, nothing.'

The steward goes away with his eyebrows mildly raised in resignation at the chance eccentricity of a passenger. The plane purrs forward. The no-smoking lights go out and the loudspeaker confirms that the passengers may now unfasten their seat-belts and smoke.

Lise unfastens hers and moves to the vacated window seat.

'I knew,' she says. 'In a way I knew there was something wrong with him.'

Bill moves to sit next to her in the middle seat and says, 'Nothing wrong with him at all. Just a fit of puritanism. He was unconsciously jealous when he saw we'd hit it off together, and he made out he was outraged as if we'd been doing something indecent. Forget him; he's probably a clerk in an insurance brokers' from the looks of him. Nasty little bureaucrat. Limited. He wasn't your type.'

'How do you know?' Lise says immediately as if responding only to Bill's use of the past tense, and, as if defying it by a counter-demonstration to the effect that the man continues to exist in the present, she half-stands to catch sight of the stranger's head, eight rows forward in a middle seat, at the other side of the aisle, now bent quietly over his reading.

'Sit down,' Bill says. 'You don't want anything to do with that type. He was frightened of your psychedelic clothes. Terrified.'

'Do you think so?'

'Yes. But I'm not.'

The stewardesses advance up the aisle bearing trays of food which they start to place before the passengers. Lise and Bill pull down the table in front of their seats to receive their portions. It is a mid-morning compromise snack composed of salami on lettuce, two green olives, a rolled-up piece of boiled ham containing a filling of potato salad and a small pickled something, all laid upon a slice of bread. There is also a round cake, swirled with white and chocolate cream, and a corner of silver-wrapped processed cheese with biscuits wrapped in cellophane. An empty plastic coffee cup stands by on each of their trays.

Lise takes from her tray the transparent plastic envelope which contains the sterilized knife, fork and spoon necessary for the meal. She feels the blade of the knife. She presses two of her fingers against the prongs of her fork. 'Not very sharp,' she says.

'Who needs them, anyway?' says Bill. 'This is awful food.'

'Oh, it looks all right. I'm hungry. I only had a cup of coffee for my breakfast. There wasn't time.'

'You can eat mine too,' says Bill. 'I stick as far as possible to a very sensible diet. This stuff is poison, full of toxics and chemicals. It's far too Yin.'

'I know,' said Lise. 'But considering it's a snack on a plane—'

'You know what Yin is?' he says.

She says, 'Well, sort of ...' in a vaguely embarrassed way, 'but it's only a snack, isn't it?'

'You understand what Yin is?'

'Well, something sort of like this—all bitty.'

'No, Lise,' he says.

'Well it's a kind of slang, isn't it? You say a thing's a bit too yin ...'; plainly she is groping.

'Yin,' says Bill, 'is the opposite of Yang.'

She giggles and, half-rising, starts searching with her eyes for the man who is still on her mind.

'This is serious,' Bill says, pulling her roughly back into her seat. She laughs and begins to eat.

'Yin and Yang are philosophies,' he says. 'Yin represents space. Its colour is purple. Its element is water. It is external. That salami is Yin and those olives are Yin. They are full of toxics. Have you ever heard of macrobiotic food?'

'No, what is it?' she says cutting into the open salami sandwich.

'You've got a lot to learn. Rice, unpolished rice is the basis of macrobiotics. I'm going to start a centre in Naples next week. It is a cleansing diet. Physically, mentally and spiritually.'

'I hate rice,' she says.

'No, you only think you do. He who hath ears let him hear.' He smiles widely towards her, he breathes into her face and touches her knee. She eats on with composure. 'I'm an Enlightenment Leader in the movement,' he says.

The stewardess comes with two long metal pots. 'Tea or coffee?' 'Coffee,' says Lise, holding out her plastic cup, her arm stretched in front of Bill. When this is done, 'For you, sir?' says the stewardess.

Bill places his hand over his cup and benignly shakes his head.

'Don't you want anything to eat, sir?' says the stewardess, regarding Bill's untouched tray.

'No, thank you,' says Bill.

Lise says, 'I'll eat it. Or at least, some of it.'

The stewardess passes on to the next row, unconcerned.

'Coffee is Yin,' says Bill.

Lise looks towards his tray. 'Are you sure you don't want that open sandwich? It's delicious. I'll eat it if you don't want it. After all, it's paid for, isn't it?'

'Help yourself,' he says. 'You'll soon change your eating habits, though, now that we've got to know each other.'

'Whatever do you eat when you travel abroad?' Lise says, exchanging his tray for hers, retaining only her coffee.

'I carry my diet with me. I never eat in restaurants and hotels unless I have to. And if I do, I choose very carefully. I go where I can get a little fish, maybe, and rice, and perhaps a bit of goat's cheese. Which are Yang. Cream cheese—in fact butter, milk, anything that comes from the cow—is too Yin. You become what you eat. Eat cow and you become cow.'

A hand, fluttering a sheet of white paper, intervenes from behind them.

They turn to see what is being offered. Bill grasps the paper. It is the log of the plane's flight, informing the passengers as to the altitude, speed and present geographical position, and requesting them to read it and pass it on.

Lise continues to look back, having caught sight of the face behind her. In the window seat, next to a comfortably plump woman and a young girl in her teens, is a sick-looking man, his eyes yellow-brown and watery, deep-set in their sockets, his face pale green. It was he who had handed forward the chart. Lise stares, her lips parted slightly, and she frowns as if speculating on the man's identity. He looks away, first out of the window, then down towards the floor, embarrassed. The woman does not change her expression, but the young girl, understanding Lise to be questioning by her stare the man behind, says, 'It's only the flight chart.' But Lise stares on. The sick-looking man looks at his companions and then down at his knees, and Lise's stare does not appear to be helping his sickness.

A nudge from Bill composes her so far that she turns and faces forward again. He says, 'It's only the flight chart. Do you want to see it?' And since she does not reply he thrusts it forward to bother it about the ears of the people in front until they receive it from his hand.

Lise starts to eat her second snack. 'You know, Bill,' she says, 'I think you were right about that crazy man who moved his seat. He wasn't my type at all and I wasn't his type. Just as a matter of interest, I mean, because I didn't take the slightest notice of him and I'm not looking to pick up strangers. But you mentioned that he wasn't my type and, of course, let me tell you, if he thought I was going to make up to him he made a mistake.'

'I'm your type,' Bill says.

She sips her coffee and looks round, glimpsing through the partition of the seats the man behind her. He stares ahead with glazed and quite unbalanced eyes, those eyes far too wide open to signify anything but some sort of mental distance from reality; he does not see Lise now, as she peers at him, or, if so, he appears to have taken a quick turn beyond caring and beyond embarrassment.

Bill says, 'Look at me, not at him.'

She turns back to Bill with an agreeable and indulgent smile. The stewardesses come efficiently collecting the trays, cluttering one upon the other. Bill, when their trays are collected, puts up first Lise's table and then his own. He puts his arm through hers.

'I'm your type,' he says, 'and you're mine. Are you planning to stay with friends?'

'No, but I have to meet somebody.'

'No chance of us meeting some time? How long are you planning to stay in the city?'

'I have no definite plans,' she says. 'But I could meet you for a drink tonight. Just a short drink.'

'I'm staying at the Metropole,' he says. 'Where will you be staying?'

'Oh, just a small place. Hotel Tomson.'

'I don't think I know Hotel Tomson.'

'It's quite small. It's cheap but clean.'

'Well, at the Metropole,' Bill says, 'they don't ask any questions.'

'As far as I'm concerned,' Lise says, 'they can ask any questions they like. I'm an idealist.'

'That's exactly what I am,' Bill says. 'An idealist. You're not offended, are you? I only meant that if we get acquainted, I think, somehow, I'm your type and you're my type.'

'I don't like crank diets,' Lise says. 'I don't need diets. I'm in good form.'

'Now, I can't let that pass, Lise,' Bill says. 'You don't know what you're talking about. The macrobiotic system is not just a diet, it's a way of life.'

She says, 'I have somebody to meet some time this afternoon or this evening.'

'What for?' he says. 'Is it a boy-friend?'

'Mind your own business,' she says. 'Stick to your yin and your yang.'

'Yin and Yang,' he says, 'is something that you've got to understand. If we could have a little time together, a little peaceful time, in a room, just talking, I could give you some idea of how it works. It's an idealist's way of life. I'm hoping to get the young people of Naples interested in it. I should think there would be many young people of Naples interested. We're opening a macrobiotic restaurant there, you know.'

Lise peers behind her again at the staring, sickly man. 'A strange type,' she says.

'With a room behind the public dining hall, a room for strict observers who are on Regime Seven. Regime Seven is cereals only, very little liquid. You take such a very little liquid that you can pee only three times a day if you're a man, two if you're a woman. Regime Seven is a very elevated regime in macrobiotics. You become like a tree. People become what they eat.'

'Do you become a goat when you eat goat's cheese?'

'Yes, you become lean and stringy like a goat. Look at me, I haven't a spare piece of fat on my body. I'm not an Enlightenment Leader for nothing.'

'You must have been eating goat's cheese,' she says. 'This man back here is like a tree, have you seen him?'

'Behind the private room for observers of Regime Seven,' Bill says, 'there will be another little room for tranquillity and quiet. It should do well in Naples once we get the youth movement started. It's to be called the Yin-Yang Young. It does well in Denmark. But middle-aged people take the diet too. In the States many senior citizens are on macrobiotics.'

'The men in Naples are sexy.'

'On this diet the Regional Master for Northern Europe recommends one orgasm a day. At least. In the Mediterranean countries we are still researching that aspect.'

'He's afraid of me,' Lise whispers, indicating with a jerk of her head the man behind her. 'Why is everybody afraid of me?'

'What do you mean? I'm not afraid of you.' Bill looks round, impatiently, and as if only to oblige her. He looks away again. 'Don't bother with him,' he says. 'He's a mess.'

Lise gets up. 'Excuse me,' she says, 'I have to go and wash.'

'See you come back,' he says.

She passes across him to the aisle, holding in her hand both her hand-bag and the paperback book she bought at the airport, and as she does so she takes the opportunity to look carefully at the three people in the row behind, the ill-looking man, the plump woman and the young girl, who sit without conversing, as it seems unconnected with each other. Lise stands for a moment in the aisle, raising the arm on which the hand-bag is slung from the wrist, so that the paperback, now held between finger and thumb, is visible. She seems to display it deliberately, as if she is one of those spies one reads about who effect recognition by pre-arranged signals and who

31

verify their contact with another agent by holding a certain paper in a special way.

Bill looks up at her and says, 'What's the matter?'

She starts moving forward, at the same time answering Bill: 'The matter?'

'You won't need that book,' Bill says.

She looks at the book in her hand as if wondering where it came from and with a little laugh hesitates by his side long enough to toss it on to her seat before she goes up the plane towards the toilets.

Two people are waiting in line ahead of her. She takes her place abstractedly, standing in fact almost even with the row where her first neighbour, the business man, is sitting. But she does not seem to be aware of him or to care in the slightest that he glances up at her twice, three times, at first apprehensively and then, as she continues to ignore him, less so. He turns a page of his newspaper and folds it conveniently for reading, and reads it without looking at her again, settling further into his seat with the slight sigh of one whose visitor has left and who is at last alone.

It has turned out that the sick-looking man is after all connected with the plump woman and the young girl who sat beside him on the plane. He is coming out of the airport building, now, not infirmly but with an air of serious exhaustion, accompanied by the woman and the girl.

Lise stands a few yards away. By her side is Bill; their luggage is on the pavement beside them. She says, 'Oh there he is!' and leaves Bill's side, running up to the sick-eyed man. 'Excuse me!' she says.

He hesitates, and makes an awkward withdrawal: two steps backward, and with the steps he seems to withdraw even more his chest, shoulders, legs and face. The plump woman looks at Lise inquiringly while the girl just stands and looks.

Lise addresses the man in English. She says, 'Excuse me, but I wondered if you wanted to share a limousine to the centre. It works out cheaper than a taxi, if the passengers agree to share, and it's quicker than the bus, of course.'

The man looks at the pavement as if inwardly going through a ghastly experience. The plump woman says, 'No, thank you. We're being met.' And touching the man on the arm, moves on. He follows, as if bound for the scaffold while the girl stares blankly at Lise before walking round and past her. But Lise quickly moves with the group, and once again confronts the man. 'I'm sure we've met somewhere before,' she says. The man rolls his head slightly as if he has toothache or a headache. 'I would be so grateful,' Lise says, 'for a lift.'

'I'm afraid—' says the woman. And just then a man in a chauffeur's uniform comes up. 'Good morning, m' lord,' he says. 'We're parked over there. Did you have a good trip?'

The man has opened his mouth wide but without making a sound; now he closes his lips tight.

'Come along,' says the plump woman, while the girl turns in an unconcerned way. The plump woman says sweetly to Lise, while brushing past her, 'I'm sorry, we can't stop at the moment. The car's waiting and we have no extra room.'

Lise shouts, 'But your luggage—you've forgotten your luggage.'

The chauffeur turns cheerily and says over his shoulder, 'No luggage, Miss, they don't bring luggage. Got all they need at the villa.' He winks and breezes about his business.

The three follow him across the street to the rows of waiting cars and are followed by other travellers who stream out of the airport building.

Lise runs back to Bill. He says, 'What are you up to?'

'I thought I knew him,' Lise says. She is crying, her tears fall heavily. She says, 'I was sure he was the right one. I've got to meet someone.'

Bill says, 'Don't cry, don't cry, people are looking. What's the matter? I don't get it.' At the same time he grins with his wide mouth as if to affirm that the incomprehensible needs must be a joke. 'I don't get it,' he says, pulling out of his pocket two men's-size paper handkerchiefs, and, selecting one, handing it to Lise. 'Who did you think he was?'

Lise wipes her eyes and blows her nose. She clutches the paper handkerchief in her fist. She says, 'It's a disappointing start to my holidays. I was sure.'

'You've got me for the next few days if you like,' Bill says. 'Don't you want to see me again? Come on, we'll get a taxi, you'll feel better in a taxi. You can't go on the bus, crying like that. I don't get it. I can give you what you want, wait and see.'

On the pavement, further up, among a cluster of people waiting for a taxi is the sturdy young man in his business suit, holding his brief-case. Lise looks listlessly at Bill, then beyond Bill, and just as listlessly takes in the man whose rosy face is turned towards her. He lifts his suitcase immediately he catches sight of her and crosses the road amongst the traffic, moving quickly away and away. But Lise is not watching him any more, she does not even seem to have remembered him.

In the taxi she laughs harshly when Bill tries to kiss her. Then she lets him kiss her, emerging from the contact with raised eyebrows as who should say, 'What next?' 'I'm your type,' Bill says.

The taxi stops at the grey stone downtown Hotel Tomson. She says, 'What's all that on the floor?' and points to a scatter of small seeds. Bill looks at them closely and then at his zipper-bag which has come unzipped by a small fraction.

'Rice,' he says. 'One of my sample packs must have burst

and this bag isn't closed properly.' He zips up the bag and says, 'Never mind.'

He takes her to the narrow swing doors and hands her suitcase to the porter. 'I'll look for you at seven in the hall of the Metropole,' he says. He kisses her on the cheek and again she raises her eyebrows. She pushes the swing door and goes with it, not looking back.

Chapter Four

A T THE HOTEL DESK she seems rather confused as if she is not quite sure where she is. She gives her name and when the concierge asks for her passport she evidently does not immediately understand, for she asks him what he wants first in Danish, then French. She tries Italian, lastly English. He smiles and responds to Italian and English, again requesting her passport in both languages.

'It is confusing,' she says in English, handing over her passport.

'Yes, you left part of yourself at home,' the concierge says. 'That other part, he is still en route to our country but he will catch up with you in a few hours' time. It's often the way with travel by air, the passenger arrives ahead of himself. Can I send you to your room a drink or a coffee?'

'No, thank you.' She turns to follow the waiting page-boy, then turns back. 'When will you be finished with my passport?'

'Any time, any time, Madam. When you come down again. When you go out. Any time.' He looks at her dress and coat, then turns to some other people who have just arrived. While the boy waits, dangling a room-key, to take her up, Lise pauses for a moment to have a good look at them. They are a family : mother, father, two sons and a small daughter all speaking German together volubly. Lise is meanwhile gazed back at by the two sons. She turns away, impatiently gesturing the page-boy towards the lift, and follows him.

In her room she gets rid of the boy quickly, and without even taking her coat off lies down on the bed, staring at the ceiling. She breathes deeply and deliberately, in and out, for a few minutes. Then she gets up, takes off her coat, and examines what there is of the room.

It is a bed with a green cotton cover, a bedside table, a rug, a dressing-table, two chairs, a small chest of drawers; there is a wide tall window which indicates that it had once formed part of a much larger room, now partitioned into two or three rooms in the interests of hotel economy; there is a small bathroom with a bidet, a lavatory, a wash-basin and a shower. The walls and a built-in cupboard have been a yellowish cream but are now dirty with dark marks giving evidence of past pieces of furniture now removed or rearranged. Her suitcase lies on a rack-table. The bedside light is a curved chromium stand with a parchment shade. Lise switches it on. She switches on the central light which is encased in a mottled glass globe; the light flicks on, then immediately flickers out as if, having served a long succession of clients without complaint, Lise is suddenly too much for it.

She tramps heavily into the bathroom and first, without hesitation, peers into the drinking-glass as if fully expecting to find what she does indeed find: two Alka-Seltzers, quite dry, having presumably been put there by the previous occupant who no doubt had wanted to sober up but who had finally lacked the power or memory to fill the glass with water and drink the salutary result.

By the side of the bed is a small oblong box bearing three pictures without words to convey to clients of all languages which bell-push will bring which room attendant. Lise examines this with a frown, as it were deciphering with the effort necessary to those more accustomed to word-reading the three pictures which represent first a frilly maid with a long-handled duster over her shoulder, next a waiter carrying a tray and lastly a man in buttoned uniform bearing a folded garment over his arm. Lise presses the maid. A light goes on in the box illuminating the picture. Lise sits on the bed and waits. Then she takes off her shoes and, watching the door for a few seconds more, presses the buttoned valet who likewise does not come. Nor does room-service after many more minutes. Lise lifts the telephone, demands the concierge and complains in a torrent that the bell-pushes bring no answer, the room is dirty, the tooth-glass has not been changed since the last guest left, the central light needs a new bulb, and that the bed, contrary to the advance specifications of her travel agency, has a too-soft mattress. The concierge advises her to press the bell for the maid.

Lise has started reciting her list over again from the beginning, when the maid does appear with a question-mark on her face. Lise puts down the receiver rather loudly and points to the light which the maid tries for herself, then, nodding her understanding of the case, makes to leave. 'Wait!' says Lise, first in English then in French, to neither of which the maid responds. Lise produces the glass with its Alka-Seltzers nestled at the bottom. 'Filthy!' Lise says in English. The maid obligingly fills the glass from the tap and hands it to Lise. 'Dirty!' Lise shouts in French. The maid understands, laughs at the happening, and this time makes a quick getaway with the glass in her hand.

Lise slides open the cupboard, pulls down a wooden hanger and throws it across the room with a clatter, then lies down on the bed. Presently she looks at her watch. It is five past one. She opens her suitcase and carefully extracts a short dressing-gown. She takes out a dress, hangs it in the cupboard, takes it off the hanger again, folds it neatly and puts it back. She takes out her sponge-bag and bedroom slippers, undresses, puts on her dressing-gown and goes into the bathroom, shutting the door. She has reached the point of taking a shower when she hears voices from her room, a scraping sound, a man's and a girl's. Putting forth her head from the bathroom door, she sees a man in light brown overalls with a pair of steps and an electric light bulb, accompanied by the maid. Lise comes out in her dressing-gown without having properly dried herself in the evident interest of protecting her hand-bag which lies on the bed. Her dressing-gown clings damply to her. 'Where is the tooth-glass?' Lise demands. 'I must have a glass for water.' The maid touches her head to denote forgetfulness and departs with a swish of her skirt, never to return within Lise's cognizance. However, Lise soon makes known her need for a drinking-glass on the telephone to the concierge, threatening to leave the hotel immediately if she doesn't get her water-glass right away.

While waiting for the threat to take effect Lise again considers the contents of her suitcase. This seems to present her with a problem, for she takes out a pink cotton dress, hangs it in the cupboard, then after hesitating for a few seconds she takes it off the hanger again, folds it carefully and lays it back in her case. It may be that she is indeed contemplating an immediate departure from the hotel. But when another maid arrives with two drinking-glasses, apologies in Italian and the explanation that the former maid had gone off duty, Lise continues to look through her belongings in a puzzled way, taking nothing further out of her suitcase.

This maid, seeing laid out on the bed the bright-coloured dress and coat in which Lise had arrived, inquires amiably if Madam is going to the beach.

'No,' says Lise.

'You American?' says the maid.

'No,' Lise says.

'English?'

'No.' Lise turns her back to continue her careful examination of her clothes in the suitcase, and the maid goes out with an unwanted air, saying. 'Good day.'

Lise is lifting the corners of her carefully packed things, as if in absent-minded accompaniment to some thought, who knows what? Then, with some access of decision, she takes off her dressing-gown and slippers and starts putting on again the same clothes that she wore on her journey. When she is dressed she folds the dressing-gown, puts the slippers back in their plastic bag, and replaces them in her suitcase. She also puts back everything that she has taken out of her sponge-bag, and packs this away.

Now she takes from an inside pocket of her suitcase a brochure with an inset map which she spreads out on the bed. She studies it closely, finding first the spot where the Hotel Tomson is situated and from there traces with her finger various routes leading into and away from the centre of the town. Lise stands, bending over it. The room is dark although it is not yet two in the afternoon. Lise switches on the central light and pores over her map.

It is marked here and there with tiny pictures which denote historic buildings, museums and monuments. Eventually Lise takes a ball-point pen from her bag and marks a spot in a large patch of green, the main parkland of the city. She puts a little cross beside one of the small pictures which is described on the map as 'The Pavilion'. She then folds up the map and replaces it in the pamphlet which she then edges in her hand-bag. The pen lies, apparently forgotten, on the bed. She looks at herself in the glass, touches her hair, then locks her suitcase. She finds the car-keys that she had failed to leave behind this morning and attaches them once more to her key-ring. She puts the bunch of keys in her hand-bag, picks up her paper-back book and goes out, locking the door behind her. Who knows her thoughts? Who can tell?

She is downstairs at the desk where, behind the busy clerks, numbered pigeon-holes irregularly contain letters, packages, the room-keys, or nothing, and above them the clock shows twelve minutes past two. Lise puts her room-key on the counter and asks for her passport in a loud voice causing the clerk whom she addresses, another clerk who sits working an adding machine, and several other people who are standing and sitting in the hotel lobby, to take notice of her.

The women stare at her clothes. They, too, are dressed brightly for a southern summer, but even here in this holiday environment Lise looks brighter. It is possibly the combination of colours—the red in her coat and the purple in her dress—rather than the colours themselves which drags attention to her, as she takes her passport in its plastic envelope from the clerk, he looking meanwhile as if he bears the whole of the eccentricities of humankind upon his slender shoulders.

Two girls, long-legged, in the very brief skirts of the times, stare at Lise. Two women who might be their mothers stare too. And possibly the fact that Lise's outfit comes so far and unfashionably below her knees gives an extra shockingness to her appearance that was not even apparent in the less up-to-date Northern city from which she set off that morning. Skirts are worn shorter here in the South. Just as, in former times, when prostitutes could be discerned by the brevity of their skirts compared with the normal standard, so Lise in her knee-covering clothes at this moment looks curiously of the street-prostitute class beside the mini-skirted girls and their mothers whose knees at least can be seen.

So she lays the trail, presently to be followed by Interpol and elaborated upon with due art by the journalists of Europe for the few days it takes for her identity to be established.

'I want a taxi,' Lise says loudly to the uniformed boy who stands by the swing door. He goes out to the street and whistles. Lise follows and stands on the pavement. An elderly woman, small, neat and agile in a yellow cotton dress, whose extremely wrinkled face is the only indication of her advanced age, follows Lise to the pavement. She, too, wants a taxi, she says in a gentle voice, and she suggests to Lise that they might share. Which way is Lise going? This woman seems to see nothing strange about Lise, so confidently does she approach her. And in fact, although this is not immediately apparent, the woman's eyesight is sufficiently dim, her hearing faint enough, to eliminate, for her, the garish effect of Lise on normal perceptions.

'Oh,' says Lise, 'I'm only going to the Centre. I've no definite plans. It's foolish to have plans.' She laughs very loudly.

'Thank you, the Centre is fine for me,' says the woman, taking Lise's laugh for acquiescence in the sharing of the taxi.

And, indeed, they do both load into the taxi and are off.

'Are you staying here long?' says the woman.

'This will keep it safe,' says Lise, stuffing her passport down the back of the seat, stuffing it down till it is out of sight.

The old lady turns her spry nose towards this operation. She looks puzzled for an instant, but soon complies with the action, moving forward to allow Lise more scope in shoving the little booklet out of sight.

'That's that,' says Lise, leaning back, breathing deeply, and looking out of the window. 'What a lovely day!'

The old lady leans back too, as if leaning on the trusting confidence that Lise has inspired. She says, 'I left my passport in the hotel, with the Desk.'

'It's according to your taste,' Lise says opening the window to the slight breeze. Her lips part blissfully as she breathes in the air of the wide street on the city's outskirts.

Soon they run into traffic. The driver inquires the precise point at which they wish to be dropped.

'The Post Office,' Lise says. Her companion nods.

Lise turns to her. 'I'm going shopping. It's the first thing I do on my holidays. I go and buy the little presents for the family first, then that's off my mind.'

'Oh, but in *these* days,' says the old lady. She folds her gloves, pats them on her lap, smiles at them.

'There's a big department store near the Post Office,' Lise says. 'You can get everything you want there.'

'My nephew is arriving this evening.'

'The traffic!' says Lise.

They pass the Metropole Hotel. Lise says, 'There's a man in that hotel I'm trying to avoid.'

'Everything is different,' says the old lady.

'A girl isn't made of cement,' Lise says, 'but everything is different now, it's all changed, believe me.'

At the Post Office they pay the fare, each meticulously contributing the unfamiliar coins to the impatient, mottled and hillocky palm of the driver's hand, adding coins little by little, until the total is reached and the amount of the tip equally agreed between them and deposited; then they stand on the pavement in the centre of the foreign city, in need of coffee and a sandwich, accustoming themselves to the lay-out, the traffic crossings, the busy residents, the ambling tourists and the worried tourists, and such of the unencumbered youth who swing and thread through the crowds like antelopes whose heads, invisibly antlered, are airborne high to sniff the prevailing winds, and who so appear to own the terrain beneath their feet that they never look at it. Lise looks down at her clothes as if wondering if she is ostentatious enough.

Then, taking the old lady by the arm, she says, 'Come and have a coffee. We'll cross by the lights.'

All perky for the adventure, the old lady lets Lise guide her to the street-crossing where they wait for the lights to change and where, while waiting, the old lady gives a little gasp and a jerk of shock; she says, 'You left your passport in the taxi!'

'Well, I left it there for safety. Don't worry,' Lise says. 'It's taken care of.'

'Oh, I see.' The old lady relaxes, and she crosses the road with Lise and the waiting herd. 'I am Mrs Fiedke,' she says. 'Mr Fiedke passed away fourteen years ago.'

In the bar they sit at a small round table, place their bags, Lise's book and their elbows on it and order each a coffee and a ham-and-tomato sandwich. Lise props up her paperback book against her bag, as it were so that its bright cover is addressed to whom it may concern. 'Our home is in Nova Scotia,' says Mrs Fiedke, 'where is yours?'

'Nowhere special,' says Lise waving aside the triviality. 'It's written on the passport. My name's Lise.' She takes her arms out of the sleeves of her striped cotton coat and lets it fall behind her over the back of the chair. 'Mr Fiedke left everything to me and nothing to his sister,' says the old lady, 'but my nephew gets everything when I'm gone. I would have liked to be a fly on the wall when she heard.'

The waiter comes with their coffee and sandwiches, moving the book while he sets them down. Lise props it up again when he has gone. She looks around at the other tables and at the people standing up at the bar, sipping coffee or fruit-juice. She says, 'I have to meet a friend, but he doesn't seem to be here.'

'My dear, I don't want to detain you or take you out of your way.'

'Not at all. Don't think of it.'

'It was very kind of you to come along with me,' says Mrs Fiedke, 'as it's so confusing in a strange place. Very kind indeed.'

'Why shouldn't I be kind?' Lise says, smiling at her with a sudden gentleness.

'Well, I'll be all right just here after we've finished our snack. I'll just take a look round and do a bit of shopping. I won't keep you, my dear.'

'You can come shopping with me,' Lise says, very genially. 'Mrs Fiedke, it's a pleasure.'

'How very kind you are!'

'One should always be kind,' Lise says, 'in case it might be

45

the last chance. One might be killed crossing the street, or even on the pavement, any time, you never know. So we should always be kind.' She cuts her sandwich daintily and puts a piece in her mouth.

Mrs Fiedke said, 'That's a very, very beautiful thought. But you mustn't think of accidents. I can assure you, I'm terrified of traffic.'

'So am I. Terrified.'

'Do you drive an automobile?' says the old lady.

'I do, but I'm afraid of traffic. You never know what crackpot's going to be at the wheel of another car.'

'These days,' says Mrs Fiedke.

'There's a department store not far from here,' Lise says. 'Want to come?'

They eat their sandwich and drink their coffee. Lise then orders a rainbow ice while Mrs Fiedke considers one way or another whether she really wants anything more, and eventually declines.

'Strange voices,' says the old lady looking round. 'Look at the noise.'

'Well, if you know the language.'

'Can you speak the language?'

'A bit. I can speak four.'

Mrs Fiedke marvels benevolently while Lise bashfully plays with crumbs on the tablecloth. The waiter brings the rainbow ice and while Lise lifts the spoon to start Mrs Fiedke says, 'It matches with your outfit.'

Lise laughs at this, longer than Mrs Fiedke had evidently expected. 'Beautiful colours,' Mrs Fiedke offers, as one might offer a cough-sweet. Lise sits before the brightly streaked ice-cream with her spoon in her hand and laughs on. Mrs Fiedke looks frightened, and more frightened as the voices of the bar stop to watch the laughing one; Mrs Fiedke shrinks into her old age, her face dry and wrinkled, her eyes gone into a far retreat, not knowing what to do. Lise stops suddenly and says, 'That was funny.'

The man behind the bar, having started coming over to their table to investigate a potential disorder, stops and turns back, muttering something. A few young men round the bar start up a mimic laugh-laugh-laugh but are stopped by the barman.

'When I went to buy this dress,' Lise says to Mrs Fiedke, 'do you know what they offered me first?—A stainless dress. Can you believe it? A dress that won't hold the stain if you drop coffee or ice-cream on it. Some new synthetic fabric. As if I would want a dress that doesn't show the stains!'

Mrs Fiedke, whose eager spirit is slowly returning from wherever it had been to take cover from Lise's laughter, looks at Lise's dress and says, 'Doesn't hold the stains? Very useful for travelling.'

'Not this dress,' Lise says, working her way through the rainbow ice; 'it was another dress. I didn't buy it, though. Very poor taste, I thought.' She has finished her ice. Again the two women fumble in their purses and at the same time Lise gives an expert's glance at the two small tickets, marked with the price, that have been left on the table. Lise edges one of them aside. 'That one's for the ice,' she says, 'and we share the other.'

'The torment of it,' Lise says. 'Not knowing exactly where and when he's going to turn up.'

She moves ahead of Mrs Fiedke up the escalator to the third floor of a department store. It is ten minutes past four by the big clock, and they have had to wait more than half an hour for it to open, both of them having forgotten about the southern shopping hours, and in this interval have walked round the block looking so earnestly for Lise's friend that Mrs Fiedke has at some point lost the signs of her initial bewilderment when this friend has been mentioned, and now shows only the traces of enthusiastic cooperation in the search. As they were waiting for the store to open, having passed the large iron-grated shutters again and again in their ambles round the block, Mrs Fiedke started to scan the passers-by.

'Would that be him, do you think? He looks very gaily dressed like yourself.'

'No, that's not him.'

'It's quite a problem, with all this choice. What about this one? No this one, I mean, crossing in front of that car? Would he be too fat?'

'No, it isn't him.'

'It's very difficult, my dear, if you don't know the cast of person.'

'He could be driving a car,' Lise had said when they at last found themselves outside the shop at the moment the gates were being opened.

They go up, now, to the third floor where the toilets are, skimming up with the escalator from which they can look down to see the expanse of each floor as the stairs depart from it. 'Not a great many gentlemen,' Mrs Fiedke remarks. 'I doubt if you'll find your friend here.'

'I doubt it too,' says Lise. 'Although there are quite a few men employed here, aren't there?'

'Oh, would he be a shop assistant?' Mrs Fiedke says.

'It depends,' says Lise.

'These days,' says Mrs Fiedke.

Lise stands in the ladies' room combing her hair while she waits for Mrs Fiedke. She stands at the basin where she has washed her hands, and, watching herself with tight lips in the glass, back-combs the white streak, and with great absorption places it across the darker locks on the crown of her head. At the basins on either side of her two other absorbed young women are touching up their hair and faces. Lise wets the tip of a finger and smooths her eyebrows. The women on either side collect their belongings and leave. Another woman, matronly with her shopping, bustles in and swings into one of the lavatory cubicles. Mrs Fiedke's cubicle still remains shut. Lise has finished tidying herself up; she waits. Eventually she knocks on Mrs Fiedke's door. 'Are you all right?'

She says again, 'Are you all right?' And again she knocks. 'Mrs Fiedke, are you all right?'

The latest comer now bursts out of her cubicle and makes for the wash-basin. Lise says to her, while rattling the handle of Mrs Fiedke's door, 'There's an old lady locked in here and I can't hear a sound. Something must have happened.' And she calls again, 'Are you all right, Mrs Fiedke?'

'Who is she?' says the other woman.

'I don't know.'

'But you're with her, aren't you?' The matron takes a good look at Lise.

'I'll go and get someone,' Lise says, and she shakes the handle one more time. 'Mrs Fiedke! Mrs Fiedke!' She presses her ear to the door. 'No sound,' she says, 'none at all.' Then she grabs her bag and her book from the wash-stand and dashes out of the ladies' room leaving the other woman listening and rattling at the door of Mrs Fiedke's cubicle.

Outside, the first department is laid out with sports equipment. Lise walks straight through, stopping only to touch one of a pair of skis, feeling and stroking the wood. A salesman approaches, but Lise has walked on, picking her way among the more populated area of School Clothing. Here she hovers over a pair of small, red fur-lined gloves laid out on the counter. The girl behind the counter stands ready to serve. Lise looks up at her. 'For my niece,' she says. 'But I can't remember the size. I think I won't risk it, thank you.' She moves across the department floor to Toys, where she spends some time examining a nylon dog which, at the flick of a switch attached to its lead, barks, trots, wags its tail and sits. Through Linen, to the down escalator goes Lise, scanning each approaching floor in her descent, but not hovering on any landing until she reaches the ground floor. Here she buys a silk scarf patterned in black and white. At a gadgets counter a salesman is demonstrating a cheap electric food-blender. Lise buys one of these, staring at the salesman when he attempts to include personal charm in his side of the bargain. He is a thin, pale man of early middle age, eager-eyed. 'Are you on holiday?' he says. 'American? Swedish?' Lise says, 'I'm in a hurry.' Resigned to his mistake, the salesman wraps her parcel, takes her money, rings up the till and gives her the change. Lise then takes the wide staircase leading to the basement. Here she buys a plastic zipper-bag in which she places her packages. She stops at the Records and Record-Players department and loiters with the small group that has gathered to hear a new pop-group disc. She holds her paperback well in evidence, her hand-bag and the new zipper-bag slung over her left arm just above the wrist, and her hands holding up the book in front of her chest like an identification notice carried by a displaced person.

> Come on over to my place
> For a sandwich, both of you,
> Any time …

The disc comes to an end. A girl with long brown pigtails is hopping about in front of Lise, continuing the rhythm with her elbows, her blue-jeans, and apparently her mind, as a newly beheaded chicken continues for a brief time, now squawklessly, its panic career. Mrs Fiedke comes up behind Lise and touches her arm. Lise says, turning to smile at her, 'Look at this idiot girl. She can't stop dancing.'

'I think I fell asleep for a moment,' Mrs Fiedke says. 'It wasn't a bad turn. I just dropped off. Such kind people. They wanted to put me in a taxi. But why should I go back to the hotel? My poor nephew won't be there till 9 o'clock tonight or maybe later; he must have missed the earlier plane. The porter was so kind, ringing up to find out the time of the next plane. All that.'

'Look at her,' Lise says in a murmur. 'Just look at her. No, wait!—She'll start again when the man puts on the next record.'

The record starts, and the girl swings. Lise says, 'Do you believe in macrobiotics?'

'I'm a Jehovah's Witness,' says Mrs Fiedke. 'But that was after Mr Fiedke passed on. I have no problems any more. Mr Fiedke cut out his sister you know, because she had no religion. She questioned. There are some things which you can't. But I know this, if Mr Fiedke was alive today he would be a Witness too. In fact he was one in many ways without knowing it.'

'Macrobiotics is a way of life,' Lise says. 'That man at the Metropole, I met him on the plane. He's an Enlightenment Leader of the macrobiotics. He's on Regime Seven.'

'How delightful!' says Mrs Fiedke.

'But he isn't my type,' Lise says.

The girl with the pigtails is dancing on by herself in front of them, and as she suddenly steps back Mrs Fiedke has to retreat out of her way. 'Is she what they call a hippy?' she says.

'There were two others on the plane. I thought they were my type, but they weren't. I was disappointed.'

'But you are to meet your gentleman soon, won't you? Didn't you say?'

'Oh, *he's* my type,' Lise says.

'I must get a pair of slippers for my nephew. Size nine. He missed the plane.'

'This one's a hippy,' says Lise, indicating with her head a

slouching bearded youth dressed in tight blue-jeans, no longer blue, his shoulders draped with an assortment of cardigans and fringed leather garments, heavy for the time of year.

Mrs Fiedke looks with interest and whispers to Lise, 'They are hermaphrodites. It isn't their fault.' The young man turns as he is touched on the shoulder by a large blue-suited agent of the store. The bearded youth starts to argue and gesticulate, but this brings another, slighter, man to his other shoulder. They lead him protesting away towards the emergency exit stairway. A slight disturbance then occurs amongst the record-hearing crowd, some of whom take the young man's part, some of whom do not. 'He wasn't doing any harm!' 'He smelt awful!' 'Who do *you* think you are?'

Lise walks off towards Televisions, followed anxiously by Mrs Fiedke. Behind them the pigtailed girl is addressing her adjacent crowd: 'They think they're in America where if they don't like a man's face they take him out and shoot him.' A man's voice barks back: 'You couldn't see his face for the hair. Go back where you came from, little whore! In this country, we ...'

The quarrel melts behind them as they come to the television sets where the few people who have been taking an interest in the salesman appear now to be torn between his calm rivulet of words and the incipient political uprising over at Records and Record-Players. Two television screens, one vast and one small, display the same programme, a wild-life documentary film which is now coming to an end; a charging herd of buffalo, large on one screen and small on the other, cross the two patches of vision while music of an unmistakably finale nature sends them on their way with equal volume from both machines. The salesman turns down the noise from the larger set, and continues to address his customers, who have now dwindled to two, meanwhile keeping an interested eye on Lise and Mrs Fiedke who hover behind.

'Would that be your gentleman?' Mrs Fiedke says, while the screens give a list of names responsible for the film, then another and another list of names. Lise says, 'I was just wondering myself. He looks a respectable type.'

'It's up to you,' says Mrs Fiedke. 'You're young and you have your life in front of you.'

A well-groomed female announcer comes on both televisions, small and large, to give out the early evening headlines, first stating that the time is 17.00 hours, then that a military coup has newly taken place in a middle-eastern country details of which are yet unknown. The salesman, abandoning his potential clients to their private deliberations, inclines his head towards Mrs Fiedke and inquires if he can help her.

'No thank you,' Lise replies in the tongue of the country. Whereupon the salesman comes close up and pursues Mrs Fiedke in English. 'We have big reductions, Madam, this week.' He looks winningly at Lise, eventually approaching to squeeze her arm. Lise turns to Mrs Fiedke. 'No good,' she says. 'Come on, it's getting late,' and she guides the old lady away to Gifts and Curios at the far end of the floor. 'Not my man at all. He tried to get familiar with me,' Lise says. 'The one I'm looking for will recognize me right away for the woman I am, have no fear of that.'

'Can you credit it?' says Mrs Fiedke looking back indignantly in the direction of Televisions. 'Perhaps we should report him. Where is the Office?'

'What's the use?' Lise says. 'We have no proof.'

'Perhaps we should go elsewhere for my nephew's slippers.'

'Do you really want to buy slippers for your nephew?' Lise says.

'I thought of slippers as a welcome present. My poor nephew—the hotel porter was so nice. The poor boy was to have arrived on this morning's flight from Copenhagen. I waited and I waited. He must have missed the plane. The porter looked up the timetable and there's another arriving tonight. I must remember not to go to bed. The plane gets in at ten-twenty but it may be eleven-thirty, twelve, before he gets to the hotel, you know.'

Lise is looking at the leather notecases, embossed with the city's crest. 'These look good,' Lise says. 'Get him one of these. He would remember all his life that you gave it to him.'

'I think slippers,' says Mrs Fiedke. 'Somehow I feel slippers. My poor nephew has been unwell, we had to send him to a clinic. It was either that or the other, they gave us no choice. He's so much better now, quite well again. But he needs rest. Rest, rest and more rest is what the doctor wrote. He takes size nine.'

Lise is playing with a corkscrew, then with a ceramic-handled cork. 'Slippers might make him feel like an invalid,' she says. 'Why don't you buy him a record or a book? How old is he?'

'Only twenty-four. It comes from the mother's side. Perhaps we should go to another shop.'

Lise leans over the counter to inquire which department is men's slippers. Patiently she translates the answer to Mrs Fiedke. 'Footwear on the third floor. We'll have to go back up. The other stores are much too expensive, they charge you what they like. The travel-folder recommends this place as they've got fixed prices.'

Up they go, once more, surveying the receding departments as they rise; they buy the slippers; they descend to the ground floor. There, near the street door, they find another gift department with a miscellany of temptations. Lise buys another scarf, bright orange. She buys a striped man's necktie, dark blue and yellow. Then, glimpsing through the crowd a rack from which dangles a larger assortment of men's ties, each neatly enfolded in transparent plastic, she changes her mind about the coloured tie she has just bought. The girl at the counter is not pleased by the difficulties involved in the refund of money, and accompanies Lise over to the rack to see if an exchange can be effected.

Lise selects two ties, one plain black knitted cotton, the other green. Then, changing her mind once more, she says, 'That green is too bright, I think.' The girl conveys exasperation, and in a manner of vexed resignation Lise says, 'All right, give me two black ties, they're always useful. Please remove the prices.' She returns to the counter where she had left Mrs Fiedke, pays the difference and takes her package. Mrs Fiedke appears from the doorway where she has been examining, by daylight, two leather notecases. A shopman, who has been hovering by, in case she should be one of those who make a dash for it, goods in hand, follows her back to the counter. He says, 'They're both very good leather.'

Mrs Fiedke says, 'I think he has one already.' She chooses a paper-knife in a sheath. Lise stands watching. She says, 'I nearly bought one of those for my boy-friend at the airport before I left. It was almost the same but not quite.' The paper-knife is made of brassy metal, curved like a scimitar. The sheath is embossed but not, like the one Lise had considered earlier in the day, jewelled. 'The slippers are enough,' Lise says.

Mrs Fiedke says, 'You're quite right. One doesn't want to spoil them.' She looks at a key-case, then buys the paper-knife.

'If he uses a paper-knife,' Lise says, 'obviously he isn't a hippy. If he were a hippy he would open his letters with his fingers.'

'Would it be too much trouble,' she says to Lise, 'to put this in your bag? And the slippers—oh, where are the slippers?'

Her package of slippers is lost, is gone. She claims to have left it on the counter while she had been to the door to compare the two leather notecases. The package has been lifted, has been taken away by somebody. Everyone looks around for it and sympathizes, and points out that it was her own fault.

'Maybe he has plenty of slippers, anyway,' Lise says. 'Is he my type of man, do you think?'

'We ought to see the sights,' says Mrs Fiedke. 'We shouldn't let this golden opportunity go by without seeing the ruins.'

'If he's my type I want to meet him,' Lise says.

'Very much your type,' says Mrs Fiedke, 'at his best.'

'What a pity he's coming so late,' Lise says. 'Because I have a previous engagement with my boy-friend. However, if he doesn't turn up before your nephew arrives I want to meet your nephew. What's his name did you say?'

'Richard. We never called him Dick. Only his mother, but not us. I hope he gets the plane all right. Oh—where's the paper-knife?'

'You put it in here,' says Lise, pointing to her zipper-bag. 'Don't worry, it's safe. Let's get out of here.'

As they drift with the outgoing shoppers into the sunny street, Mrs Fiedke says, 'I hope he's on that plane. There was some talk that he would go to Barcelona first to meet his mother, then on here to meet up with me. But I wouldn't play. I just said No! No flying from Barcelona, I said. I'm a strict believer, in fact, a Witness, but I never trust the airlines from those countries where the pilots believe in the afterlife. You are safer when they don't. I've been told the Scandinavian airlines are fairly reliable in that respect.'

Lise looks up and down the street and sighs. 'It can't be long now. My friend's going to turn up soon. He knows I've come all this way to see him. He knows it, all right. He's just waiting around somewhere. Apart from that I have no plans.'

'Dressed for the carnival!' says a woman, looking grossly at Lise as she passes, and laughing as she goes her way, laughing without possibility of restraint, like a stream bound to descend whatever slope lies before it.

Chapter Five

IT IS IN MY MIND,' says Mrs Fiedke; 'it is in my mind and I can't think of anything else but that you and my nephew are meant for each other. As sure as anything, my dear, you are the person for my nephew. Somebody has got to take him on, anyhow, that's plain.'

'He's only twenty-four,' considers Lise. 'Much too young.'

They are descending a steep path leading from the ruins. Steps have been roughly cut out of the earthy track, outlined only by slats of wood which are laid at the edge of each step. Lise holds Mrs Fiedke's arm and helps her down one by one.

'How do you know his age?' says Mrs Fiedke.

'Well, didn't you tell me, twenty-four?' Lise says.

'Yes, but I haven't seen him for quite a time you know. He's been away.'

'Maybe he's even younger. Take care, go slowly.'

'Or it could be the other way. People age when they've had unpleasant experiences over the years. It just came to me while we were looking at those very interesting pavements in that ancient temple up there, that poor Richard may be the very man that you're looking for.'

'Well, it's your idea,' says Lise, 'not mine. I wouldn't know till I'd seen him. Myself, I think he's around the corner somewhere, now, any time.'

'Which corner?' The old lady looks up and down the street which runs below them at the bottom of the steps.

'Any corner. Any old corner.'

'Will you feel a presence? Is that how you'll know?'

'Not really a presence,' Lise says. 'The lack of an absence,

57

that's what it is. I know I'll find it. I keep on making mistakes, though.' She starts to cry, very slightly sniffing, weeping, and they stop on the steps while Mrs Fiedke produces a trembling pink face-tissue from her bag for Lise to dab her eyes with and blow her nose on. Sniffing, Lise throws the shredded little snitch of paper away and again takes Mrs Fiedke's arm to resume their descent. 'Too much self-control, which arises from fear and timidity, that's what's wrong with them. They're cowards, most of them.'

'Oh, I always believe *that*,' says Mrs Fiedke. 'No doubt about it. The male sex.'

They have reached the road where the traffic thunders past in the declining sunlight.

'Where do we cross?' Lise says, looking to right and left of the overwhelming street.

'They are demanding equal rights with us,' says Mrs Fiedke. 'That's why I never vote with the Liberals. Perfume, jewellery, hair down to their shoulders, and I'm not talking about the ones who were born like that. I mean, the ones that can't help it should be put on an island. It's the others I'm talking about. There was a time when they would stand up and open the door for you. They would take their hat off. But they want their equality today. All I say is that if God had intended them to be as good as us he wouldn't have made them different from us to the naked eye. They don't want to be all dressed alike any more. Which is only a move against us. You couldn't run an army like that, let alone the male sex. With all due respects to Mr Fiedke, may he rest in peace, the male sex is getting out of hand. Of course, Mr Fiedke knew his place as a man, give him his due.'

'We'll have to walk up to the intersection,' Lise says, guiding Mrs Fiedke in the direction of a distant policeman surrounded by a whirlpool of traffic. 'We'll never get a taxi here.'

'Fur coats and flowered poplin shirts on their backs,' says

Mrs Fiedke as she winds along, conducted by Lise this way and that to avoid the oncoming people in the street. 'If we don't look lively,' she says, 'they will be taking over the homes and the children, and sitting about having chats while we go and fight to defend them and work to keep them. They won't be content with equal rights only. Next thing they'll want the upper hand, mark my words. Diamond earrings, I've read in the paper.'

'It's getting late,' says Lise. Her lips are slightly parted and her nostrils and eyes, too, are a fragment more open than usual; she is a stag scenting the breeze, moving step by step, inhibiting her stride to accommodate Mrs Fiedke's pace, she seems at the same time to search for a certain air-current, a glimpse and an intimation.

'I clean mine with toothpaste when I'm travelling,' confides Mrs Fiedke. 'The better stuff's in the bank back home, of course. The insurance is too high, isn't it? But you have to bring a few bits and pieces. I clean them with my toothbrush and ordinary toothpaste, then I rub them with the hand-towel. They come up very nicely. You can't trust the jewellers. They can always take them out and replace them with a fake.'

'It's getting late,' says Lise. 'There are so many faces. Where did all the faces come from?'

'I ought to take a nap,' says Mrs Fiedke, 'so that I won't feel too tired when my nephew arrives. Poor thing. We have to leave for Capri tomorrow morning. All the cousins, you know. They've taken such a charming villa and the past will never be mentioned. My brother made that clear to them. I made it clear to my brother.'

They have reached the circular intersection and turn into a side-street where a few yards ahead at the next corner there is a taxi-rank occupied by one taxi. This one taxi is taken by someone else just as they approach it.

'I smell burning,' says Mrs Fiedke as they stand at the corner waiting for another taxi to come along. Lise sniffs, her lips parted and her eyes moving widely from face to face among the passers-by. Then she sneezes. Something has happened to the people in the street, they are looking round, they are sniffing too. Somewhere nearby a great deal of shouting is going on.

Suddenly round the corner comes a stampede. Lise and Mrs Fiedke are swept apart and jostled in all directions by a large crowd composed mainly of young men, with a few smaller, older and grimmer men, and here and there a young girl, all yelling together and making rapidly for somewhere else. 'Tear-gas!' someone shouts and then a lot of people are calling out, 'Tear-gas!' A shutter on a shop-front near Lise comes down with a hasty clatter, then the other shops start closing for the day. Lise falls and is hauled to her feet by a tough man who leaves her and runs on.

Just before it reaches the end of the street which joins the circular intersection the crowd stops. A band of grey-clad policemen come running towards them, in formation, bearing tear-gas satchels and with their gas-masks at the ready. The traffic on the circular intersection has stopped. Lise swerves with her crowd into a garage where some mechanics in their overalls crouch behind the cars and others take refuge underneath a car which is raised on a cradle in the process of repair.

Lise fights her way to a dark corner at the back of the garage where a small red Mini-Morris, greatly dented, is parked behind a larger car. She wrenches at the door, forcefully, as if she expects it to be locked. It opens so easily as to throw her backwards, and as soon as she regains her balance she gets inside, locks herself in and puts her head down between her knees, breathing heavily, drawing in the smell of petrol blended faintly with a whiff of tear-gas. The demonstrators form up in the garage and are presently discovered and routed out by the police. Their exit is fairly orderly bar the shouting.

Lise emerges from the car with her zipper-bag and her

hand-bag, looking to see what damage has been done to her clothes. The garage men are vociferously commenting on the affair. One is clutching his stomach proclaiming himself poisoned and vowing to sue the police for the permanent damage caused him by tear-gas. Another, with his hand to his throat, gasps that he is suffocating. The others are cursing the students whose gestures of solidarity, they declare in the colourful derisive obscenities of their mother-tongue, they can live without. They stop when Lise limps into view. There are six of them in all, including a young apprentice and a large burly man of middle age, without overalls, wearing only a white shirt and trousers and the definite air of the proprietor. Apparently seeing in Lise a tangible remnant of the troubles lately visited upon his garage, this big fellow turns on her to vent his fury with unmastered hysteria. He advises her to go home to the brothel where she came from, he reminds her that her grandfather was ten times cuckolded, that she was conceived in some ditch and born in another; after adorning the main idea with further illustrations he finally tells her she is a student.

Lise stands somewhat entranced; by her expression she seems almost consoled by this outbreak, whether because it relieves her own tensions after the panic or whether for some other reason. However, she puts a hand up to her eyes, covering them, and in the language of the country she says, 'Oh please, please. I'm only a tourist, a teacher from Iowa, New Jersey. I've hurt my foot.' She drops her hand and looks at her coat which is stained with a long black oily mark. 'Look at my clothes,' Lise says. 'My new clothes. It's best never to be born. I wish my mother and father had practised birth-control. I wish that pill had been invented at the time. I feel sick, I feel terrible.'

The men are impressed by this, one and all. Some are visibly cheered up. The proprietor turns one way and another with arms outstretched to call the whole assembly to witness his dilemma. 'Sorry, lady, sorry. How was I to know ? Pardon me, but I thought you were one of the students. We have a lot of trouble from the students. Many apologies, lady. Was there something we can do for you? I'll call the First Aid. Come and sit down, lady, over here, inside my office, take a seat. You see the traffic outside, how can I call the ambulance through the traffic? Sit down, lady.' And, having ushered her into a tiny windowed cubicle, he sits Lise in its only chair beside a small sloping ledger-desk and thunders at the men to get to work.

Lise says, 'Oh please don't call anyone. I'll be all right if I can get a taxi to take me back to my hotel.'

'A taxi! Look at the traffic!'

Outside the archway that forms the entrance to the garage, there is a dense block of standing traffic.

The proprietor keeps going to look up and down the street and returning to Lise. He calls for benzine and a rag to clean Lise's coat. No rag clean enough for the purpose can be found and so he uses a big white handkerchief taken from the breast pocket of his coat which hangs behind the door of the little office. Lise takes off her black-stained coat and while he applies his benzine-drenched handkerchief to the stain, making it into a messy blur, Lise takes off her shoes and rubs her feet. She puts one foot up on the the slanting desk and rubs. 'It's only a bruise,' she says, 'not a sprain. I was lucky. Are you married?'

The big man says, 'Yes, lady, I'm married,' and pauses in his energetic task to look at her with new, appraising and cautious eyes. 'Three children—two boys, one girl,' he says. He looks through the office at his men who are occupied with various jobs and who, although one or two of them cast a swift glance at Lise with her foot up on the desk, do not give any sign of noticing any telepathic distress signals their employer might be giving out.

The big man says to Lise, 'And yourself? Married?'

'I'm a widow,' Lise says, 'and an intellectual. I come from a family of intellectuals. My late husband was an intellectual. We had no children. He was killed in a motor accident. He was a bad driver, anyway. He was a hypochondriac, which means that he imagined that he had every illness under the sun.'

'This stain,' said the man, 'won't come out until you send the coat to the dry-cleaner.' He holds out the coat with great care, ready for her to put on; and at the same time as he holds it as if he means her, temptress in the old-fashioned style that she is, to get out of his shop, his eyes are shifting around in an undecided way.

Lise takes her foot off the desk, stands, slips into her shoes, shakes the skirt of her dress and asks him, 'Do you like the colours?'

'Marvellous,' he says, his confidence plainly diminishing in confrontation with this foreign distressed gentlewoman of intellectual family and conflicting appearance.

'The traffic's moving. I must get a taxi or a bus. It's late,' Lise says, getting into her coat in a business-like manner.

'Where are you staying, lady?'

'The Hilton,' she says.

He looks round his garage with an air of helpless, antici-patory guilt. 'I'd better take her in the car,' he mutters to the mechanic nearest him. The man does not reply but makes a slight movement of the hand to signify that it isn't for him to give permission.

Still the owner hesitates, while Lise, as if she had not over-heard his remarks, gathers up her belongings, holds out her hand and says 'Good-bye. Thank you very much for helping me.' And to the rest of the men she calls 'Good-bye, good-bye, many thanks!'

The big man takes her hand and holds on to it tightly as if his grasp itself was a mental resolution not to let go this unforeseen, exotic, intellectual, yet clearly available treasure.

He holds on to her hand as if he was no fool, after all. 'Lady, I'm taking you to your hotel in the car. I couldn't let you go out into all this confusion. You'll never get a bus, not for hours. A taxi, never. The students, we have the students only to thank.' And he calls sharply to the apprentice to bring out his car. The boy goes over to a brown Volkswagen. 'The Fiat!' bellows his employer, whereupon the apprentice moves to a dusty cream-coloured Fiat 125, passes a duster over the outside of the windscreen, gets into it and starts to manoeuvre it forward to the main ramp.

Lise pulls away her hand and protests. 'Look, I've got a date. I'm late for it already. I'm sorry, but I can't accept your kind offer.' She looks out at the mass of slowly-moving traffic, the queues waiting at the bus-stops, and says, 'I'll have to walk. I know my way.'

'Lady,' he says, 'no argument. It's my pleasure.' And he draws her to the car where the apprentice is now waiting with the door open for her.

'I really don't know you,' Lise says.

'I'm Carlo,' says the man, urging her inside and shutting the door. He gives the grinning apprentice a push that might mean anything, goes round to the other door, and drives slowly towards the street, slowly and carefully finding a gap in the line of traffic, working his way in to the gap, blocking the oncoming vehicles for a while until finally he joins the stream.

It is also getting dark, as big Carlo's car alternately edges and spurts along the traffic. Carlo meanwhile denouncing the students and the police for causing the chaos. When they come at last to a clear stretch Carlo says, 'My wife I think is no good. I heard her on the telephone and she didn't think I was in the house. I heard.'

'You must understand,' Lise says, 'that anything at all that is overheard when the speaker doesn't know you're listening takes on a serious note. It always sounds far worse than their actual intentions are.'

'This was bad,' mutters Carlo. 'It's a man. A second cousin of hers. I made a big trouble for her that night, I can tell you. But she denied it. How could she deny it? I heard it.'

'If you imagine,' Lise says, 'that you are justifying any anticipations you may have with regards to me, you're mistaken. You can drop me off here, if you like. Otherwise, you can come and buy me a drink at the Hilton Hotel, and then it's good night. A soft drink. I don't take alcohol. I've got a date that I'm late for already.'

'We go out of town a little way,' says Carlo. 'I know a place. I brought the Fiat, did you see? The front seats fold back. Make you comfortable.'

'Stop at once,' Lise says. 'Or I put my head out of the window and yell for help. I don't want sex with you. I'm not interested in sex. I've got other interests and as a matter of fact I've got something on my mind that's got to be done. I'm telling you to stop.' She grabs the wheel and tries to guide it into the curb.

'All right, all right,' he says, regaining control of the car which has swerved a little with Lise's interference. 'All right. I'm taking you to the Hilton.'

'It doesn't look like the Hilton road to me,' Lise says. The traffic lights ahead are red but as there is very little traffic about on this dark, wide residential boulevard, he chances it and skims across. Lise puts her head out of the window and yells for help.

He pulls up at last in a side lane where, back from the road, there are the lights of two small villas; beyond that the road is a mass of stony crevices. He embraces her and kisses her mightily while she kicks him and tries to push him off, gurgling her protests. When he stops for breath he says, 'Now we put back the seats and do it properly.' But already she has jumped out of the car and has started running towards the gate of one of the houses, wiping her mouth and screaming, 'Police! Call the police!' Big Carlo overtakes her at the gate. 'Quiet!' he says. 'Be quiet, and get into the car. Please. I'll take you back, I promise. Sorry, lady, I haven't done any harm at all to you, have I? Only a kiss, what's a kiss.'

She runs and makes a grab for the door of the driver's seat, and as he calls after her, 'The other door!' she gets in, starts up, and backs speedily out of the lane. She leans over and locks the other door just in time to prevent him from opening it. 'You're not my type in any case,' she screams. Then she starts off, too quickly for him to be able to open the back door he is now grabbing at. Still he is running to catch up, and she yells back at him, 'If you report this to the police I'll tell them the truth and make a scandal in your family.' And then she is away, well clear of him.

She spins along in expert style, stopping duly at the traffic lights. She starts to sing softly as she waits:

> Inky-pinky-winky-wong
> How do you like your potatoes done?
> A little gravy in the pan
> For the King of the Cannibal Islands.

Her zipper-bag is on the floor of the car. While waiting for the lights to change she lifts it on to the seat, unzips it and looks with a kind of satisfaction at the wrapped-up objects of different shape, as it might be they represent a good day's work. She comes to a crossroad where some traffic accumulates. Here, a policeman is on duty and as she passes at his bidding she pulls up and asks him the way to the Hilton.

He is a young policeman. He bends to give her the required direction.

'Do you carry a revolver?' Lise says. He looks puzzled and

fails to answer before Lise adds, 'Because, if you did, you could shoot me.'

The policeman is still finding words when she drives off, and in the mirror she can see him looking at the retreating car, probably noting the number. Which in fact he is doing, so that, on the afternoon of the following day, when he has been shown her body, he says, 'Yes, that's her. I recognize the face. She said, "If you had a revolver you could shoot me."' Which is to lead to many complications in Carlo's private life when the car is traced back to him, he being released by the police only after six hours of interrogation. A photograph of Carlo and also a picture of his young apprentice who holds a lively press conference of his own, moreover will appear in every newspaper in the country.

But now, at the Hilton Hotel her car is held up just as it enters the gates in the driveway. There is a line of cars ahead, and beyond them a group of policemen. Two police cars are visible in the parking area on the other side of the entrance. The rest of the driveway is occupied by a line of four very large limousines each with a uniformed driver standing by.

The police collect on either side of the hotel doorway, their faces picked out by the bright lights, while there emerge down the steps from the hotel two women who seem to be identical twins, wearing black dresses and high-styled black hair, followed by an important-looking Arabian figure, sheikh-like in his head-dress and robes, with a lined face and glittering eyes, who descends the steps with a floating motion as if his feet are clearing the ground by an inch or two; he is flanked by two smaller bespectacled, brown-faced men in business-like suits. The two black-dressed women stand back with a respectful housekeeperly bearing while the robed figure approaches the first limousine; and the two men draw back too, as he enters the recesses of the car. Two black-robed women with the lower parts of their faces veiled and their heads shrouded in drapery then make their descent, and behind them another pair appear, men-servants with arms raised, bearing aloft numerous plastic-enveloped garments on coat-hangers. Still in pairs, further components of the retinue appear, each two moving in such unison that they seem to share a single soul or else two well-rehearsed parts in the chorus of an opera by Verdi. Two men wearing western clothes but for their red fezes are duly admitted to one of the waiting limousines and, as Lise gets out of her car to join the watchers, two ramshackle young Arabs with rumpled grey trousers and whitish shirts end the procession, bearing two large baskets, each one packed with oranges and a jumbo-sized vacuum-flask which stands slightly askew among the fruit, like champagne in an ice-bucket.

A group of people who are standing near Lise on the driveway, having themselves got out of their held-up taxis and cars, are discussing the event: 'He was here on vacation. I saw it on the television. There's been a coup in his country and he's going back.'—'Why should he go back?'—'No, he won't go back, believe me. Never.'—'What country is it? I hope it doesn't affect us. The last time there was a coup my shares regressed so I nearly had a breakdown. Even the mutual funds …'

The police have gone back to their cars, and escorted by them the caravan goes its stately way.

Lise jumps back into Carlo's car and conducts it as quickly as possible to the car park. She leaves it there, taking the keys. Then she leaps into the hotel, eyed indignantly by the doorman who presumably resents her haste, her clothes, the blurred stain on her coat, the rumpled aspect that she has acquired in the course of the evening and whose built-in computer system rates her low on the spending scale.

Lise makes straight for the ladies' toilets and while there, besides putting her appearance to rights as best she can, she takes a comfortable chair in the soft-lit rest-room and considers, one by one, the contents of her zipper-bag which she lays on a small table beside her. She feels the outside of the box containing the food-blender and replaces it in her bag. She also leaves unopened a soft package containing the neckties, but, having rummaged in her hand-bag for something which apparently is not there, she brings forth her lipstick and with it she writes on the outside of the soft package, 'Papa'. There is an unsealed paper bag which she peers into; it is the orange scarf. She puts it back into place and takes out another bag containing the black and white scarf. She folds this back and with her lipstick she traces on the outside of the bag in large capitals, 'Olga'. Another package seems to puzzle her. She feels round it with half-closed eyes for a moment, then opens it up. It contains the pair of men's slippers which Mrs Fiedke had mislaid in the shop having apparently in fact put them in Lise's bag. Lise wraps them up again and replaces them. Finally she takes out her paperback book and an oblong package which she opens. This is a gift-box containing the gilded paper-opener in its sheath, also Mrs Fiedke's property.

Lise slowly returns the lipstick to her handbag, places the book and the box containing the paper-knife on the table beside her, places the zipper-bag on the floor, then proceeds to examine the contents of her hand-bag. Money, the tourist folder with its inset map of the city, the bunch of six keys that she had brought with her that morning, the keys of Carlo's car, the lipstick, the comb, the powder compact, the air ticket. Her lips are parted and she leans back in a relaxed attitude but that her eyes are too wide open for restfulness. She looks again at the contents of her hand-bag. A notecase with paper money, a purse with loose change. She gathers herself together in such an abrupt manner that the toilet attendant who has been sitting vacantly in a corner by the wash-basins starts to her feet. Lise packs up her belongings. She puts the paper-knife box back in the zipper-bag, carefully tucking it down the side, and zips the bag up. Her hand-bag is also packed tidily again, except for the bunch of six keys that she had brought on her travels. She holds the book in her hand, and, placing the bunch of six keys with a clatter on the plate left out for the coins, the attendant's reward, she says to the woman, 'I won't be needing these now.' Then, with her zipper-bag, her book, her hand-bag, her hair combed and her face cleaned up, she swings out of the door and into the hotel lounge. The clock above the reception desk says nine thirty-five. Lise makes for the bar, where she looks round. Most of the tables are occupied by chattering groups. She sits at a vacant but rather out-of-the-way table, orders a whisky, and bids the tentative waiter hurry. 'I've got a train to catch.' She is served with the drink together with a jug of water and a bowl of peanuts. She drenches the whisky with water, sips a small part of it and eats all the peanuts. She takes another small sip from her glass, and, leaving it nearly full, stands up and motions the waiter to bring her bill. She pays for this high-priced repast with a note taken from her bag and tells the waiter to keep the change, which amounts to a very high tip. He accepts it with incredulous grace and watches her as she leaves the bar. He, too, will give his small piece of evidence to the police on the following day, as will also the toilet attendant, trembling at the event which has touched upon her life without the asking.

Lise stops short in the hotel lounge and smiles. Then without further hesitation she goes over to a group of armchairs, only one of which is occupied. In it sits a sickly-looking man. Bending over him deferentially to listen to something the man is saying is a uniformed chauffeur who presently turns to go, waved away by the seated man, just as Lise approaches.

'There you are!' says Lise. 'I've been looking for you all day. Where did you get to?'

The man shifts to look at her. 'Jenner's gone to have a bite. Then we're off back to the villa. Damn nuisance, coming back in to town all this way. Tell Jenner he's got half-an-hour. We must be off.'

'He'll be back in a minute,' Lise says. 'Don't you remember we met on the plane?'

'The Sheikh. Damn rotters in his country have taken over behind his back. Now he's lost his throne or whatever it is he sits on. I was at school with him. Why did he ring me up? He rang me up. On the telephone. He brings me back to town all this way and when we get here he says he can't come to the villa after all, there's been a coup.'

'I'll take you back to the villa,' Lise says. 'Come on. get in the car with me. I've got a car outside.'

The man says, 'Last time I saw the Sheikh it was '38. He came on safari with me. Rotten shot if you know anything about big game. You've got to wait for the drag. They call it the drag, you see. It kills its prey and drags it into the bush then you follow the drag and when you know where it's left its prey you're all right. The poor bloody beast comes out the next day to eat its prey, they like it high. And you only have a few seconds. You're here and there's another fellow there and a third over here. You can't shoot from here, you see, because there's another hunter there and you don't want to shoot him. You have to shoot from over here or over there. And the Sheikh, I've known him for years, we were at school together, the bloody fool shot and missed it by five feet from a fifteen-foot range.'

His eyes look straight ahead and his lips quiver.

'You're not my type after all,' Lise says. 'I thought you were, but I was away out.'

'What? Want a drink? Where's Jenner?'

She gathers up the handles of her bags, picks up her book and looks at him and through him as if he were already a distant memory and leaves without a good-bye, indeed as if she had said good-bye to him long ago.

She brushes past a few people at the vestibule who look at her with the same casual curiosity with which others throughout the day have looked at her. They are mainly tourists; one exceptional sight among so many others does not deflect their attention for very long. Outside, she goes to the car park where she has left Carlo's car, and does not find it.

She goes up to the doorman. 'I've lost my car. A Fiat 125. Have you seen anyone drive off with a Fiat?'

'Lady, there are twenty Fiats an hour come in and out of here.'

'But I parked it over there less than an hour ago. A cream Fiat, a bit dirty, I've been travelling.'

The doorman sends a page-boy to find the parking attendant who presently comes along in a vexed mood since he has been called from conversation with a more profitable client. He owns to having seen a cream-coloured Fiat being driven away by a large fat man whom he had presumed to be the owner.

'He must have had extra keys,' says Lise.

'Didn't you see the lady drive in with it?' the doorman says.

'No, I didn't. The royalty and the police were taking up all my time, you know that. Besides, the lady didn't say anything to me, to look after her car.'

Lise says, opening her bag, 'Well, I meant to give you a tip later. But I'll give you one now.' And she holds out to him the keys of Carlo's car.

The doorman says, 'Look, lady, we can't take responsibility for your car. If you want to see the porter at the desk he can ring the police. Are you staying at the hotel?'

'No,' says Lise. 'Get me a taxi.'

'Have you got your licence?' says the parking attendant.

'Go away,' Lise says. 'You're not my type.' He looks explosive. Another of tomorrow's witnesses.

The porter is meanwhile busy helping some newcomers

out of a taxi. Lise calls out to the taxi-driver, who nods his agreement to take her on.

As soon as the passengers are out, Lise leaps into the taxi.

The parking attendant shouts, 'Are you sure it was your own car, lady?'

She throws Carlo's keys out of the window on to the gravel and directs the taxi to the Hotel Metropole with tears falling over her cheeks.

'Anything the matter, lady?' says the driver.

'It's getting late,' she says, weeping. 'It's getting terribly late.'

'Lady, I can't go faster. See the traffic.'

'I can't find my boy-friend. I don't know where he's gone.'

'You think you'll find him at the Metropole?'

'There's always a chance,' she says. 'I make a lot of mistakes.'

Chapter Six

THE CHANDELIERS OF THE METROPOLE, dispensing a vivid glow upon the just and unjust alike, disclose Bill the macrobiotic seated gloomily by a table near the entrance. He jumps up when Lise enters and falls upon her with a delight that impresses the whole lobby, and in such haste that a plastic bag that he is clutching, insufficiently sealed, emits a small trail of wild rice in his progress towards her.

She follows him back to his seat and takes a chair beside him. 'Look at my coat,' she says. 'I got mixed up in a student demonstration and I'm still crying from the effect of tear-gas. I had a date at the Hilton for dinner with a very important Sheik but I was too late, as I went to buy him a pair of slippers for a present. He'd gone on safari. So he wasn't my type, anyway. Shooting animals.'

'I'd just about given you up,' says Bill. 'You were to be here at seven. I've been getting desperate.' He takes her hand, smiling with glad flashes of teeth and eyes. 'You wouldn't have been so unkind as to have dinner with someone else, would you? I'm hungry.'

'And my car got stolen,' she says.

'What car?'

'Oh, just a car.'

'I didn't know you had a car. Was it a hired car?'

'You know nothing whatsoever about me,' she says.

'Well I've got a car,' he said. 'A friend has lent me it. I'm taking it to Naples as soon as possible to get started on the Yin-Yang Young Culture Centre. I'm opening with a lecture called "The World—Where is it Going?" That will be a general introduction to the macrobiotic way of life. It'll bring in the kids, all right.'

'It's getting late,' she says.

'I was nearly giving you up,' he says, squeezing her hand. 'I was just about to go out and look for another girl. I'm queer for girls. It has to be a girl.'

'I'll have a drink,' she says. 'I need one.'

'Oh no, you won't. Oh no, you won't. Alcohol is off the diet. You're coming to supper with me at a house I know.'

'What kind of a house?' she says.

'A macrobiotic family I know,' he says. 'They'll give us a good supper. Three sons, four daughters, the mother and father, all on macrobiotics. We'll have rice with carrots followed by rice biscuits and goat's cheese and a cooked apple. No sugar allowed. The family eat at six o'clock, which is the orthodox system, but the variation that I follow lets you eat late. That way, we'll get through to the young. So we'll go there and heat up a meal. Come on!'

She says, 'That tear-gas is still affecting me.' Tears brim in her eyes. She gets up with him and lets him, trailing rice, lead her past every eye of the Metropole lobby into the street, up the road, and into a small black utility model which is parked there.

'It's wonderful,' says Bill as he starts up the car, 'to think we're together again at last.'

'I must tell you,' says Lise, sniffing, 'that you're not my type. I'm sure of it.'

'Oh, you don't know me! You don't know me at all.'

'But I know my type.'

'You need love,' he says with a hand on her knee.

She starts away from him. 'Take care while you're driving. Where do your friends live?'

'The other side of the park. I must say, I feel hungry.'

'Then hurry up,' she says.

'Don't you feel hungry?'

'No, I feel lonely.'

'You won't be lonely with me.'

They have turned into the park.

'Turn right at the end of this road,' she says. 'There should be a road to the right, according to the map. I want to look at something.'

'There are better places farther on.'

'Turn right, I say.'

'Don't be nervy,' he says. 'You need to relax. The reason why you're so tense, you've been eating all the wrong things and drinking too much. You shouldn't have more than three glasses of liquid a day. You should pass water not more than twice a day. Twice for a woman, three times for a man. If you need to go more than that it means you're taking in too much fluid.'

'Here's the road. Turn right.'

Bill turns right, going slowly and looking about him. He says, 'I don't know where this leads to. But there's a very convenient spot farther up the main road.'

'What spot?' she says. 'What spot are you talking about?'

'I haven't had my daily orgasm. It's an essential part of this particular variation of the diet, didn't I tell you? Many other macrobiotic variations have it as an essential part. This is one of the main things the young Neapolitans must learn.'

'If you think you're going to have sex with me,' she says, 'you're very much mistaken. I have no time for sex.'

'Lise!' says Bill.

'I mean it,' she says. 'Sex is no use to me, I assure you.' She gives out her deep laughter.

The road is dimly lit by lamps posted at far intervals. Bill is peering to right and left.

'There's a building over there,' she says. 'That must be the Pavilion. And the old villa behind—they say in the brochure that it's to be restored and turned into a museum. But it's the famous Pavilion that I want.'

At the site of the Pavilion several cars and motor bicycles are parked. Another road converges, and a band of teenaged boys and girls are languidly leaning against trees, cars and anything else that can prop them up, looking at each other.

'There's nothing doing here,' says Bill.

'Stop, I want to get out and look around.'

'Too many people. What are you thinking of?'

'I want to see the Pavilion, that's all.'

'Why? You can come by daylight. Much better.'

Some iron tables are scattered on the ground in front of the Pavilion, a graceful three-storey building with a quaint gilded frieze above the first level of the façade.

Bill parks the car near the others, some of which are occupied by amorous couples. Lise jumps out as soon as the car stops. She takes with her the hand-bag leaving the zipper-bag and her book in the car. He runs after her, putting an arm round her shoulders, and says, 'Come on, it's getting late. What do you want to see?'

She says, 'Will your rice be safe in the car? Have you locked it?'

He says, 'Who's going to steal a bag of rice?'

'I don't know,' says Lise, making her way along the path which leads to the Pavilion. 'Maybe those young people might feel very intensely about rice.'

'The movement hasn't got started yet, Lise,' says Bill. 'And red beans are also allowed. And sesame-flour. But you can't expect people to know about it till you tell them.'

The ground floor of the Pavilion is largely glass-fronted. She goes up to it and peers in. There are bare café tables and chairs piled high in the classic fashion of restaurants closed for the night. There is a long counter and a coffee machine at the far end, with an empty glass sandwich-bar. There is nothing else except an expanse of floor, which in the darkness can only be half-seen, patterned in black-and-white chequered pavements. Lise cranes and twists to see the ceiling which obscurely seems to be painted with some classical scene; the hind-leg of a horse and one side of a cupid are all that is visible.

Still she peers through the glass. Bill tries to draw her away, but again she starts to cry. 'Oh,' she says, 'the inconceivable sorrow of it, those chairs piled up at night when you're sitting in a café, the last one left.'

'You're getting morbid, dear,' says Bill. 'Darling, it's all a matter of chemistry. You've been eating toxic foods and neglecting the fact that there are two forces in the world, centrifugal which is Yin and centripetal which is Yang. Orgasms are Yang.'

'It makes me sad,' she says. 'I want to go home, I think. I want to go back home and feel all that lonely grief again. I miss it so much already.'

He jerks her away and she calls out, 'Stop it! Don't do that!' A man and two women who are passing a few yards away turn to look, but the young group pays no attention.

Bill gives a deep sigh. 'It's getting late,' he says, pinching her elbow.

'Let me go, I want to look round the back. I've got to see how things are round here, it's important.'

'You'd think it was a bank,' Bill says, 'that you were going to do a stick-up in tomorrow. Who do you think you are? Who do you think I am?' He follows her as she starts off round the side of the building, examining the track. 'What do you think you're doing?'

She traverses the side of the building and turns round to the back where five large dust-bins stand waiting for tomorrow's garbage-men, who will also find Lise, not far off, stabbed to death. At this moment, a disturbed cat leaves off its foraging at one of the half-closed dust-bins and flows into an adjacent blackness.

Lise surveys the ground earnestly.

'Look,' says Bill. 'Lise, darling, over by the hedge. We're all right.'

He pulls her towards a hedge separating the back yard of the Pavilion from a foot-path which can be seen through a partly-open iron gate. A band of very tall fair young men all speaking together in a Scandinavian-sounding language passes by and stops to watch and comment buoyantly on the tussle that ensues between Bill and Lise, she proclaiming that she doesn't like sex and he explaining that if he misses his daily orgasm he has to fit in two the next day. 'And it gives me indigestion,' he says, getting her down on the gravel behind the hedge and out of sight, 'two in one day. And it's got to be a girl.'

Lise now shrieks for help in four languages, English, French, Italian and Danish. She throws her hand-bag into the hedge; then, 'He's taken my purse!' she cries in four languages. 'He's gone off with my hand-bag!' One of the onlookers tries to creak open the stiff iron gate, but meantime another has started to climb it, and gets over.

'What's going on?' he says to Lise in his own language. 'We're Swedes. What's wrong?'

Bill who has been kneeling to hold her down gets up and says, 'Go away. Clear off. What do you think's going on?'

But Lise has jumped to her feet and shouts in English that she never saw him before in her life, and that he is trying to rob her, and rape her. 'I just got out of my car to look at the Pavilion, and he jumped on me and dragged me here,' she screams, over and over again in four languages. 'Get the police!'

The other men have come into the yard. Two of them take hold of Bill who grins, trying hard to convince them that this turmoil is Lise's joke. One of them says he is going to find a policeman. Lise says, 'Where's my bag? He's got rid of it somewhere. What has he done with it?' Then, in a burst of spontaneous composure she says, quietly, 'I'm going to find a policeman, too,' and walks off to the car. Most of the other parked cars have gone, as have also the young loiterers. One of the Swedes runs after her, advising her to wait till his friend brings a policeman.

'No, I'm going to the police-station right away,' she says in a calm voice as she gets in and shuts the door. She has already made off, already thrown the bag of wild rice out of the window, when the police arrive on the scene. They hear the Swedes' account, they listen to Bill's protests, they search for Lise's bag, and find it. Then they ask Bill what the girl's name was since she was, as he claims, a friend of his. 'Lise,' he says. 'I don't know her other name. We met on the plane.'

They take Bill into custody anyway, mercifully for him as it turns out, since in the hours logically possible for the murder of Lise on that spot Bill is safely in a police cell, equally beyond suspicion and the exercise of his diet.

Chapter Seven

IT IS LONG PAST MIDNIGHT when she arrives at the Hotel Tomson which stands like the only living thing in the shuttered street. Lise parks the little black car in a spot near the entrance, takes her book and her zipper-bag and enters the hall.

At the desk the night-porter is on duty, the top three buttons of his uniform unfastened to reveal his throat and the top of his under-vest, a sign that the deep night has fallen and the tourists have gone to bed. The porter is talking on the desk telephone which links with the bedrooms. Meanwhile the only other person in the hall, a youngish man in a dark suit, stands before the desk with a brief-case and a tartan hold-all by his side.

'Please don't wake her. It isn't at all necessary at this late hour. Just show me my room—'

'She's on her way down. She says to tell you to wait, she's on her way.'

'I could have seen her in the morning. It wasn't necessary. It's so late.' The man's tone is authoritative and vexed.

'She's wide awake, sir,' says the porter. 'She was very definite that we were to let her know as soon as you arrived.'

Excuse me,' Lise says to the porter, brushing against the dark-suited man as she comes up to the desk beside him. 'Would you like a book to read?' She holds out her paperback. 'I don't need it any more.'

'Oh, thanks, Miss,' says the porter, good-naturedly taking the book and holding it at arm's length before his eyes the better to see what the book is all about. Meanwhile the new arrival, having been jostled by Lise, turns to look at her. He starts, and bends to pick up his bags.

Lise touches him on the arm. 'You're coming with me,' she says.

'No,' he says, trembling. His round face is pink and white, his eyes are wide open with fear. He looks neat in his business suit and white shirt, as he did this morning when Lise first followed and then sat next to him on the plane.

'Leave everything,' says Lise. 'Come on, it's getting late.'

She starts propelling him to the door.

'Sir!' calls the porter. 'Your aunt's on her way—'

Lise, still holding her man, turns at the door and calls back, 'You can keep his luggage. You can have the book as well; it's a whydunnit in q-sharp major and it has a message: never talk to the sort of girls that you wouldn't leave lying about in your drawing-room for the servants to pick up.' She leads her man towards the door.

There, he puts up some resistance: 'No, I don't want to come. I want to stay. I came here this morning, and when I saw you here I got away. I want to get away.' He pulls back from her.

'I've got a car outside," says Lise, and pushes open the narrow swing-door. He goes with her as if he is under arrest. She takes him to the car, lets go of his arm, gets into the driver's seat and waits while he walks round the front of the car and gets in beside her. Then she drives off with him at her side.

He says, 'I don't know who you are. I never saw you before in my life.'

'That's not the point,' she says. 'I've been looking for you all day. You've wasted my time. What a day! And I was right first time. As soon as I saw you this morning I knew that you were the one. You're my type.'

He is trembling. She says, 'You were in a clinic. You're Richard. I know your name because your aunt told me.'

He says, 'I've had six years' treatment. I want to start afresh. My family's waiting to see me.'

'Were the walls of the clinic pale green in all the rooms? Was there a great big tough man in the dormitory at night, patrolling up and down every so often, just in case?'

'Yes,' he says.

'Stop trembling,' she says. 'It's the madhouse tremble. It will soon be over. Before you went to the clinic how long did they keep you in prison?'

'Two years,' he said.

'Did you strangle or stab?'

'I stabbed her, but she didn't die. I never killed a woman.'

'No, but you'd like to. I knew it this morning.'

'You never saw me before in your life.'

'That's not the point,' Lise says. 'That's by the way. You're a sex maniac.'

'No, no,' he says. 'That's all over and past. Not any more.'

'Well you won't have sex with me,' Lise says. She is driving through the park and turns right towards the Pavilion. Nobody is in sight. The wandering groups are null and void, the cars have gone away.

'Sex is normal,' he says. 'I'm cured. Sex is all right.'

'It's all right at the time and it's all right before,' says Lise, 'but the problem is afterwards. That is, if you aren't just an animal. Most of the time, afterwards is pretty sad.'

'You're afraid of sex,' he says, almost joyfully, as if sensing an opportunity to gain control.

'Only of afterwards,' she says. 'But that doesn't matter any more.'

She pulls up at the Pavilion and looks at him. 'Why are you shaking?' she says. 'It will soon be over.' She reaches for her zipper-bag and opens it. 'Now,' she says, 'let's be lucid about this. Here's a present from your aunt, a pair of slippers. You can pick them up later.' She throws them on the back seat and pulls out a paper bag. She peers into it. 'This is Olga's scarf,' she says, putting it back in the bag.

'A lot of women get killed in the park,' he says, leaning back; he is calmer now.

'Yes, of course. It's because they want to be.' She is searching in the bag.

'Don't go too far,' he says quietly.

'I'll leave that to you,' she says and brings out another paper bag. She peers in and takes out the orange scarf. 'This is mine,' she says. A lovely colour by daylight.' She drapes the scarf round her neck.

'I'm getting out,' he says, opening the door on his side. 'Come on.'

'Wait a minute,' she says. 'Just wait a minute.'

'A lot of women get killed,' he says.

'Yes, I know, they look for it.' She brings out the oblong package, tears off the wrapping and opens the box that contains the curved paper-knife in its sheath. 'Another present for you,' she says. 'Your aunt bought it for you.' She takes the knife from the box which she throws out of the window.

He says, 'No, they don't want to be killed. They struggle. I know that. But I've never killed a woman. Never.'

Lise opens the door and gets out with the paper-knife in her hand. 'Come on, it's getting late,' she says. 'I know the spot.'

The morning will dawn, and by the evening the police will place in front of him the map marked with an X at the point where the famous Pavilion is located, the little picture.

'You made this mark.'

'No I didn't. She must have made it herself. She knew the way. She took me straight there.'

They will reveal, bit by bit, that they know his record. They will bark, and exchange places at the desk. They will come and go in the little office, already beset by inquietude and fear, even before her identity is traced back to where she came from. They will try soft speaking, they will reason with him in their secret dismay that the evidence already coming in seems to confirm his story.

'The last time you lost control of yourself didn't you take the woman for a drive in the country?'

'But this one took me. She made me go. She was driving. I didn't want to go. It was only by chance that I met her.'

'You never saw her before?'

'The first time was at the airport. She sat beside me on the plane. I moved my seat. I was afraid.'

'Afraid of what? What frightened you?'

Round and round again will go the interrogators, moving slowly forward, always bearing the same questions like the whorling shell of a snail.

Lise walks up to the great windows of the Pavilion and presses close to look inside, while he follows her. Then she walks round the back and over to the hedge.

She says, 'I'm going to lie down here. Then you tie my hands with my scarf; I'll put one wrist over the other, it's the proper way. Then you'll tie my ankles together with your neck-tie. Then you strike.' She points first to her throat. 'First here,' she says. Then, pointing to a place beneath each breast, she says, 'Then here and here. Then anywhere you like.'

'I don't want to do it,' he says, staring at her. 'I didn't mean this to happen. I planned everything to be different. Let me go.'

She takes the paper-knife from its sheath, feels the edge and the point, and says that it isn't very sharp but it will do. 'Don't forget,' she says, 'that it's curved.' She looks at the engraved sheath in her hand and lets it fall carelessly from her fingers. 'After you've stabbed,' she says, 'be sure to twist it upwards or it may not penetrate far enough.' She demonstrates the movement with her wrist. 'You'll get caught, but at least you'll have the illusion of a chance to get away in the car. So afterwards, don't waste too much time staring at what you have done, at what you have done.' Then she lies down on the gravel and he grabs at the knife.

'Tie my hands first,' she says, crossing her wrists. 'Tie them with the scarf.'

He ties her hands, and she tells him in a sharp, quick voice to take off his necktie and bind her ankles.

'No,' he says, kneeling over her, 'not your ankles.'

'I don't want any sex,' she shouts. 'You can have it afterwards. Tie my feet and kill, that's all. They will come and sweep it up in the morning.'

All the same, he plunges into her, with the knife poised high.

'Kill me,' she says, and repeats it in four languages.

As the knife descends to her throat she screams, evidently perceiving how final is finality. She screams and then her throat gurgles while he stabs with a turn of his wrist exactly as she instructed. Then he stabs wherever he likes and stands up, staring at what he has done. He stands staring for a while and then, having started to turn away, he hesitates as if he had forgotten something of her bidding. Suddenly he wrenches off his necktie and bends to tie her ankles together with it.

He runs to the car, taking his chance and knowing that he will at last be taken, and seeing already as he drives away from the Pavilion and away, the sad little office where the police clank in and out and the typewriter ticks out his unnerving statement: 'She told me to kill her and I killed her. She spoke in many languages but she was telling me to kill her all the time. She told me precisely what to do. I was hoping to start a new life.' He sees already the gleaming buttons of the policemen's uniforms, hears the cold and the confiding, the hot and the barking voices, sees already the holsters and epaulets and all those trappings devised to protect them from the indecent exposure of fear and pity, pity and fear.